Puffin Books

no-name bird

'It must have a name . . . It's such a beautiful bird. A great bird. A fighter,' said Jose.
Adolfo shouted. 'No name, no name! It's a fighting bird! It must not have a name.'

East Timor. 1975.

Jose Rodrigus was fourteen years old when the Indonesians came.

This is his moving and extraordinary story.

It is the story of his unusual relationship with Uncle Adolfo and the fighting bird they train. As the politics of their country erupt and the people, including Jose's family, have their daily lives changed for ever, Jose is caught up in adventure and danger. In the middle of the turmoil, Uncle Adolfo buys a bird to train for the local cockfights. And the bird becomes Jose's symbol of courage and strength, a magnificent fighting cock whom his uncle said must never have a name.

Because courage has no other name.

And it is the thing that Jose clings to as his world is torn apart.

Also by Josef Vondra

Non-fiction
Timor Journey
Hong Kong – City Without a Country
Taiwan – The Other China

Fiction
Paul Zwilling

Josef Vondra

no-name bird

Puffin Books

An Professor Anna Vodicka, Vienna, fuer ihre Liebe,
Hilfe und Beistand

Puffin Books
Penguin Books Australia Ltd
487 Maroondah Highway, PO Box 257
Ringwood, Victoria 3134, Australia
Penguin Books Ltd
Harmondsworth, Middlesex, England
Penguin Putnam Inc.
375 Hudson Street, New York, New York 10014, USA
Penguin Books Canada Limited
10 Alcorn Avenue, Toronto, Ontario, Canada, M4V 3B2
Penguin Books (N.Z.) Ltd
Cnr Rosedale and Airborne Roads, Albany, Auckland, New Zealand
Penguin Books (South Africa) (Pty) Ltd
5 Watkins Street, Denver Ext 4, 2094, South Africa
Penguin Books India (P) Ltd
11, Community Centre, Panchsheel Park, New Delhi, 110 017, India

First published by Penguin Books Australia, 2000

1 3 5 7 9 10 8 6 4 2

Text copyright © Josef Vondra, 2000

All rights reserved. Without limiting the rights under copyright reserved above,
no part of this publication may be reproduced, stored in or introduced into a
retrieval system, or transmitted, in any form or by any means (electronic, mechanical,
photocopying, recording or otherwise), without the prior written permission of
both the copyright owner and the above publisher of this book.

Designed by Debra Billson, Penguin Design Studio
Cover photography © Eduardo Garcia/FPG/Austral
Digital imaging by Paul Fenton
Typeset in 11/15 pt Sabon by Post Pre-press Group, Brisbane, Queensland
Made and printed in Australia by Australian Print Group, Maryborough, Victoria

National Library of Australia
Cataloguing-in-Publication data:

Vondra, Josef, 1941– .
No-name bird.

ISBN 0 14 028317 X.

I. Title.

A823.3

www.puffin.com.au/

'Courage in your own.'

Adam Lindsay Gordon

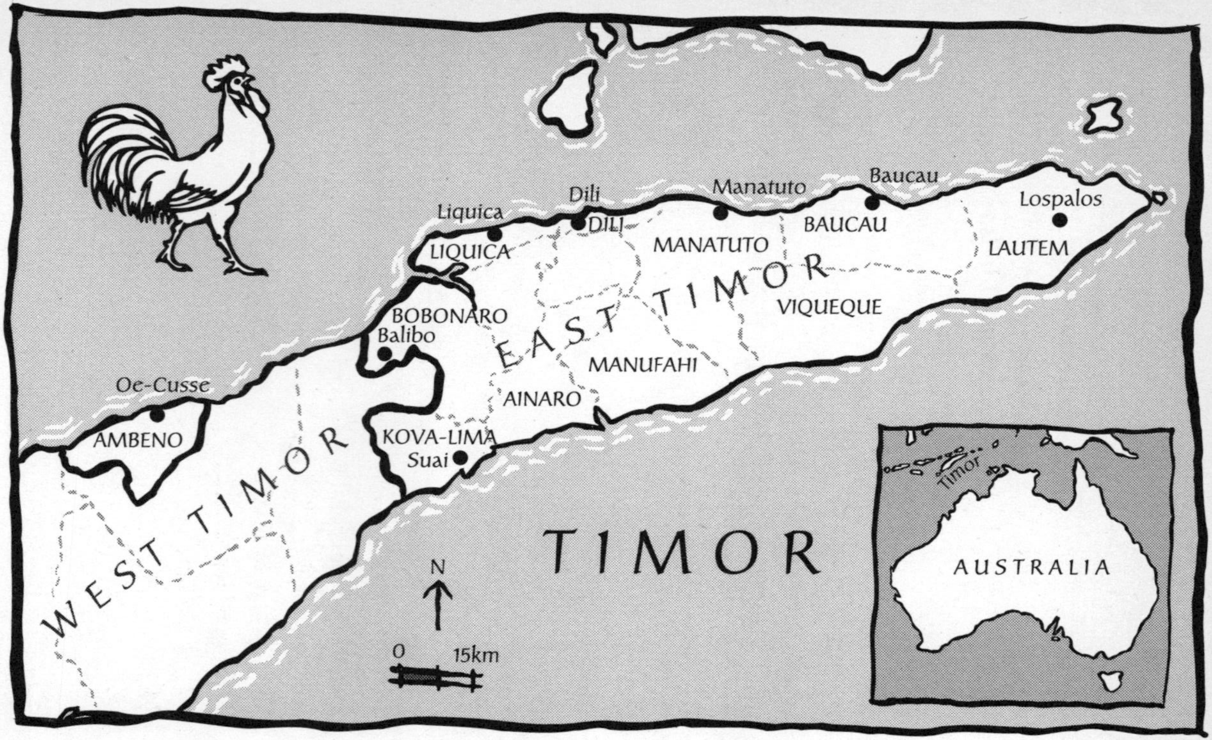
TIMOR
EAST TIMOR
WEST TIMOR
Liquica
LIQUICA
Dili
DILI
Manatuto
MANATUTO
Baucau
BAUCAU
Lospalos
LAUTEM
VIQUEQUE
MANUFAHI
AINARO
BOBONARO
Balibo
KOVA-LIMA
Suai
Oe-Cusse
AMBENO
N
0
15km
Timor
AUSTRALIA

Contents

Prologue – The Feather

1	The Fight at the Marketplace	3
2	The Warrior's Son	14
3	The Blonde Lady	22
4	Theresa Asks for Help	34
5	The Chef de Posto	39
6	Adolfo and the War	47
7	Lemonade	51
8	The Tree of Life	59
9	Rendezvous at Batugade	69
10	Flight to Balibo	80
11	Adolfo Buys a Bird	86
12	Tongues Wagging	94
13	Training	99
14	No-Name Bird	103
15	Carmillo	111
16	Old Wong Considers a Request	118
17	The Challenge	124
18	The First Round	130
19	The Blonde Lady is Angry	135
20	Under Fire	141
21	Trying to Find Safety	150
22	The Flag	156
23	Marconi	160
24	Fretilin	166
25	Run for the Airport	174

Epilogue – The Letter from Timor

The Feather

From the window of his office, Doctor Jose Cavaco da Costa Rodrigus had a clear view of the Praça. He sighed, and took another sip from the demitasse of coffee balanced in the palm of his hand. The view never failed to inspire. He often stood here, in the early morning, at the open window with the warm summer's air flooding into his spacious legal chambers, and he simply let his eyes take in the beauty of it. He sighed again. He felt that from here he understood what Lisbon was all about, a reflection of its colonial greatness. More than a few clients had remarked that it was one of the best views of the city.

He put the cup and saucer down on the desk. The tourist season was in full swing, and even this early, the Praça was already crowded.

There was a soft knock. Joao, the junior clerk, entered with the mail.

After whispering a polite, 'Bon Dia, Doctor', the young

man moved across the room and held out a stack of envelopes. Right on top was a multi-coloured airmail sleeve. Joao held the Doctor's eyes. 'It's from Timor', he said. 'I knew you would want to read it first.'

Doctor Rodrigus nodded. 'Thank you, Joao. I'm grateful.' He sat down at his desk and by the time the young man had closed the door, he had already slit the envelope carefully with an ornamental paper knife.

As he read, his hand instinctively moved across the polished surface of the desk, fingers searching for a large plastic paperweight amongst all the legal briefs. Without looking up from the letter, he turned the thick plastic slab over and over in his fingers.

Finally, he moved his eyes from the letter to the paperweight he held.

The bright morning light caught the iridescent colours of a single large cock's feather, suspended in plastic, in all its splendour.

1

The Fight at the Marketplace

As he did every Sunday, Jose Rodrigus stood naked on a stone slab at the rear of the house just before dawn, and soaped his body with a cloth. The house was silent. He shivered a little in the cool air. Carefully, methodically, he lathered his chest and tried to reach as much of his back as he could, then brushed the cloth downwards over his legs to his ankles. Make sure you clean the back of the neck, he heard his mother's voice. Look at you, nearly fourteen and I still have to tell you that! Clean, clean, I want those ears to be clean! Folding the cloth over a finger, he rubbed the flesh behind his left ear, then the right. Satisfied, he began ladling water over himself with a cupped hand. To dry himself he used an old towel a tourist had forgotten at the pool.

He padded back into the house and dressed. In a spotless white shirt and dark blue shorts, he was just about to open the front door when Adolfo came out of his room, khaki shorts hanging from his bony frame. He rubbed a palm over the crinkled skin of his face; his eyes shone feverish in their sockets.

'You'll be late for mass,' he said crisply.

'Will you be at the tree this afternoon?'

'Where else would I be?'

'Will you bet on the birds?'

'What else would I do?'

'Tio . . .?'

Adolfo cut him short. 'Go, go, no more talk. You'll be late.'

Jose walked along the gravelled road which led past the Posada, the inn where all the tourists stayed. Then the road curved around the pool and continued towards the marketplace. His mind was aflame with a hundred thoughts. He didn't want to think about anything else but the cockfights that he and Adolfo attended every Sunday. He thought about squatting with Adolfo under the jacaranda tree where they always sat, and helping his uncle select the birds to bet on. They would talk, watch the fights . . .

The bell in the church tower tolled.

Jose started to run. Father Petri would be angry if he was late! It took at least ten minutes to change into his altar boy vestments.

But as Jose moved about the altar helping Father Petri, he couldn't concentrate on the service. He kept thinking about the cockfights. Vivid images flashed before his eyes, birds circling in the fighting pit, the heady dust of the excited spectators, the noise that rose above the crowd . . .

There was more than the usual number of people in the church and between the second and third mass, Father Petri looked at Jose, his brow wrinkled in concern, and said that he may not have enough wafers for communion. 'Difficult times,' the old Goan priest said, shaking his head. There was sadness in his voice. 'It always brings them out.'

There was a lot of talk about the troubles lately, Jose thought. Everyone talked about the 'troubles'.

The government in Portugal had changed, the voices said. The old order had fallen and the new regime wanted change. Change too was coming to Timor. The voices talked about the new politics, the formation of parties, that the Portuguese would leave Timor. People whispered about all this and were afraid.

'The troubles make people frightened,' Jose said.

The old priest shot him a quick glance, then shrugged. 'Change will lead to turbulence.'

'Because the Portuguese leave?'

'There are many hot-heads about. Once the army leaves, the hot-heads will have their day.'

'But why would the Portuguese leave, Father?'

Father Petri adjusted his clothes. He peeked through the curtain of the tiny vestry. People were already moving into the church for the third mass of the day. 'Keeping colonies is expensive, Jose. Especially for a poor country like Portugal. The young men don't want to fight on foreign soil, not any more. Everyone is tired of war.' He laughed – a short, nervous cough. 'The Portuguese have been in Timor for nearly four hundred years, and now, when it is no longer convenient, they will leave. From one day to the next, just like that.' He snapped his fingers. A loud crack echoed in the vestry. 'Politics is like that, Jose. The fate of people is of no consequence.'

Jose too adjusted his vestments and handed Father Petri the communion wafers.

'Will the hot-heads make trouble when the Portuguese leave?'

'They are already doing a lot of shouting. Some want Timor to be independent, others want the Indonesians to come. Everyone has an opinion.' Father Petri gestured with his hand. 'Jose, let's leave the troubles to the others, eh? It's time to serve God!'

At communion during the third mass, the railing in front of the altar was packed with white, brown and yellow faces. As Father Petri bent over them and placed the white host on their tongues, he angrily mouthed several times: 'Concentrate, Jose, concentrate!' But Jose kept forgetting things and his mind wandered back to the fighting pit and the troubles.

His mother and stepfather usually attended this last mass. More people came to the late mass than any other on Sunday and afterwards, moodily, Jose went home with his parents. There were, as usual, many questions tumbling about in his head over breakfast that morning.

'Papa? Are you frightened about the troubles?' he asked.

'Everyone's frightened of the troubles,' Miguel said brusquely.

'Don't worry yourself with them, Jose,' Theresa said. 'They are not your concern. Your concern is breakfast and homework!'

On Sunday, Jose usually had to study a couple of hours before he was allowed to go to the fights at the marketplace. His mother sat at the end of the kitchen table, still dressed in her Sunday best of a blue blouse and black skirt, and watched carefully as her son tucked into two slices of thick, white bread and a fried egg. Jose was always ravenous after mass. He cut the white around the egg, then dipped the crust of the bread into the deep-yellow yolk. When that too had gone, he wiped the traces of egg with the last of the bread.

Theresa's forehead was crinkled into an annoyed scowl. Her tongue clicked irritably. 'Eat properly. Cockfights, that's all you and Adolfo ever talk about. A waste of time!' She brushed a hand over her face. 'You should be learning, reading books, not going out with those idiots to fight their birds! You'll end up just like them. A nothing!'

She often talked like that; the troubles were getting to her, Jose thought. Though her lips were pulled down at the corners and Jose knew she would be angry, she sighed deeply, and reluctantly said a soft 'yes' when he finally asked if he could go.

A little distance ahead of their house, the road looped and then continued straight through the middle of the collection of Chinese stores and palm-thatched huts which made up Baucau. Beyond the cluster of houses, however, another road branched off the main gravel one. It swung past the Baucau administrative building, a long, grey-brown barrack-like construction, past the half-finished market – slabs of concrete, steel support mesh, naked pillars stretching towards the sky, three giant archways empty and overgrown with weeds. His stepfather Miguel always said it would have been one of Timor's grandest buildings had the government not run out of money. Right in front of the ruins was the town's cockpit, and to one side was a large spreading jacaranda tree under which the open market was held.

Jose ran all the way down to the market. Adolfo was already sitting under another jacaranda, a much smaller one to the other side of the cockpit. He was slowly, thoughtfully sucking on one of his rolled clove-spiced cigarettes. His eyes were slits. As was his custom every Sunday, he wore a freshly washed T-shirt, clean khaki shorts and the sandals he reserved for this special day. One item which never changed was the floppy canvas hat.

Without speaking, Jose squatted down beside his uncle.

They watched in silence as, on the other side of the cockpit, the women packed up the fruits and vegetables, the jars of oil, the other goods that they had offered for sale. Then, one by one, they slowly moved off until they were all gone. The concrete slabs of the unfinished market building cast a long shadow over the cockpit.

Jose's heart beat impatiently as he watched the men drift towards the ring. A few carried birds, some pure white, others with feathers coloured by the rainbow. And in the shade of the massive jacaranda tree, the betting started.

'Tio . . .?' Jose tried to talk to his uncle several times.

'Shhh!'

'Sorry!'

The first fights started and they had a clear view from where they sat. The pit was a perfect circle, bordered by a low concrete wall which came up to Jose's knees. The floor of the pit was tightly packed trampled earth, as hard as rock. Jose always thought it was red because of the blood spilled by the birds, but Adolfo said it was the natural colour of the soil.

Most of the birds belonged to Rikki, the garage hand at the Posada. During weekdays Rikki kept the inn's only vehicle, a battered Land Rover, in perfect running order and it was also his job to drive the tourists about, usually east to Ioro, where people built their houses up on stilts and sold beautifully woven mats. But on Sunday, Rikki became the most cursed and envied man in Baucau. And the most arrogant.

Jose saw him coming, pushing through the crowd, a thin-faced, small man dressed in green military shorts and a faded T-shirt. People said Rikki had no love in his heart because his Portuguese father had been sent to Timor for stealing things in Lisbon. 'Now Rikki steals our money at the cockpit here in Baucau!' Adolfo said. Like father, like son.

Two men followed Rikki, carrying birds, and for a moment Jose thought they were going to walk right past, but just as Rikki was above them, he twisted his head sideways and shouted down: 'Aee-i! You've come to give me money.' He flipped his head back and laughed loudly. 'See, I have some good fights for you. Have a look at these beauties!'

Jose looked up, and was about to spring to his feet. It was better to face Rikki's evil while he was standing. Adolfo's hand restrained him. Studying the end of his cigarette, he said simply: 'They are good birds.'

Jose flicked his gaze from one bird to the other. Like all in Rikki's stable, the birds' combs had been shaven down to a thin, pink line. It made them look vicious, dangerous, mean.

'Why don't you bet, Adolfo? Luck might be with you today.'

'I'll bet when I want to.'

'Bet now, Adolfo! These birds are good. They come from Laga.'

'Which one is yours, Rikki?'

Rikki laughed. 'Ah, you should know.'

'Which one?'

Rikki shook his head.

The men now crowded around them. Jose felt more uncomfortable, squatting there with all their faces looking down.

'Yes, I'll bet,' Adolfo said and pulled out a handful of escudo notes.

'Don't Uncle, don't bet!' Jose whispered frantically. 'You know the birds will lose!'

'Quiet! This is not the business of the young.'

Rikki yelled: 'Dollars, dollars!'

Adolfo shook his head. 'Escudos!'

'Escudos, ha!' Rikki flicked his head contemptuously.

Adolfo carefully placed his escudo notes on the ground before him. Everyone looked at them.

One of the Chinese bookies pushed through the crowd and in one smooth movement, scooped up the notes. Later, side by side, Jose and Adolfo stood at the edge of the ring and watched their bird lose. Jose had to bite back tears as he saw the bird Tio Adolfo had placed money on held up by the matcher. It looked so small and vulnerable.

'It is too small, Tio,' Jose said.

'Sssshhhhhh . . . the small ones are often the best. They have more fighting spirit because they are small.'

'But this one is *too* small. Much too small!'

'Quiet!'

The bird had little chance. As soon as the matcher placed it on the ground in the centre of the ring, it danced about trying to manoeuvre itself into a position where it could attack. But the other bird was bigger, and more aggressive. I can sense its fear, Jose thought. He wanted to run out into the pit and scoop up the bird. All around people were shouting. 'Tio! Tio!' Jose added but Adolfo didn't hear. Or didn't want to hear.

Both birds had been fitted with steel spurs, eight-centimetre-long razor sharp knives, one each attached to their natural spurs with coloured cotton. The aggressive bird flew up and hovered over their bird – an instant only. It stalled, then down came the knife cruelly cutting. The defeat took only a few moments.

Adolfo turned away and shrugged his shoulder. 'It doesn't matter which bird wins, they both belonged to Rikki.'

It nearly always ended like this, Adolfo losing his money. Jose couldn't remember the last time Tio Adolfo had had a win.

As they moved through the crowd looking for another bird to bet on, Rikki shouted above the noise: 'Hey, Aee-ie! You missed again, Adolfo. Even Jose would do better than you!'

Suddenly Jose noticed Carmillo, Rikki's son, standing to one side of his father. Jose and Carmillo sat in the same class, and Jose hated him. A curious contrast, the fat bulk of the son nearly as tall as the abnormally thin body of the father. When Carmillo's eyes locked onto his, he saw a chubby hand come up, the fingers formed in a gesture. Carmillo mouthed an obscenity.

Jose felt Adolfo's firm hand on his arm, pulling him along until they were under the jacaranda tree again. With deliberate slowness, Adolfo took the tobacco pouch from his pocket, opened it with both hands, then rolled a few strands of the clove-flavoured tobacco into a shred of newspaper.

Jose glanced up and there was Rikki, arms flapping about his body. He wasn't going to give in so easily.

Why didn't Adolfo *do* something? Jose wondered. Shout back at Rikki. Anything but take his ridicule like that. Adolfo had fought against the Japanese during the war. Why didn't he jump up against Rikki?

'Tio?'

'Quiet!'

'Stupid, fat, turd-faced Carmillo,' Jose mouthed.

'Quiet! They are only words!'

'*Tio* . . .'

Rikki was now in full flight. Hands on hips, he stood above them, shouting: 'Ah, mad Adolfo with his war-time stories! Heeei-eh. Adolfo and his Tree of Life!' Blowing his cheeks into bulbs, he squirted a stream of scarlet betel nut juice, accurately, between his uncle's knees. It made a dull thump as it hit the dirt and spread to form a star.

As Adolfo didn't chew he couldn't retaliate. Jose

watched with sadness and frustrated anger as his uncle's head dropped down on his chest.

'*Tio*! Don't let him do this!'

'This has nothing to do with you!'

'See!' Rikki raved, pointing a finger down at them, his face distorted with fury. Why was he so angry with Adolfo? Jose wondered.

'Look at Adolfo sitting there, Adolfo with his stories about the war, Adolfo who's only good for cleaning the pool for the tourists but can't pick a winner among the birds.'

Something snapped in Adolfo then. Jose watched as his uncle's body suddenly began to tremble. He was on his feet and with Jose beside him, he stepped towards Rikki. 'You're evil, evil, evil,' he hissed. 'The Unni-spirit has you by the tail.'

Jose too was on his feet. 'Yes, evil, evil!' he shouted at Carmillo.

The fat face twisted. 'I'll get you, I'll get you later,' Carmillo hissed.

'If you can catch me, fat one!' Jose hissed back.

Ignoring the exchange between Carmillo and Jose, Rikki laughed at Adolfo. 'No, it is you the spirit has! It is your tail the Unni-spirit has!' His eyes watered at the humour of it all and he laughed again, slapping his hand hard against his thigh. The men around him started to laugh too because laughter is something which must be shared.

Then Jose saw the whole brown-yellow wall of faces encircling them explode in a loud boom of open mouths and pink throats.

2

The Warrior's Son

Jose noticed something different about Adolfo today as soon as they started up the broad and gravelled road on their way to the pool. There was a spring in his uncle's step, and every so often he shifted the long pole with the net on the end from one shoulder to the other with a quick flip. At the same time he kicked his heels in a small skip.

'Anything wrong, Tio?'

Adolfo switched the pole yet again. 'You'll see!'

Their leather sandals made a soft crunching noise on the gravel. Several times Jose looked up at Adolfo's grinning face.

The sun was already high but hidden behind dense, steamy clouds: it was very hot and humid. As they passed the tourist Posada, Toni the gardener was sweeping the stone steps. Jose eased the straps of the canvas bag he carried from his left shoulder to the right.

Toni stopped his sweeping when he saw them and

placed both hands on top of his broom, his legs apart, watching. He grinned a toothless grin. 'Bon Dia!' he called.

'Bon Dia!' Jose and Adolfo returned.

'You have visitors, Adolfo!' Toni pointed towards the pool further along the road. 'Ah, important visitors.'

'I have indeed!'

'They are waiting for you at the pool.'

Adolfo didn't interrupt the rhythm of his walk. 'Then I'd better hurry!' He readjusted his floppy canvas hat which had slipped over one eye. 'Make sure the steps are nice and clean for the tourists, Toni!'

Toni lifted his broom and stabbed at the sky. 'Hi-eeey! You make sure the pool is as clean as these steps!'

'I'll do that!'

A little further down the road, Jose asked: 'Who are the visitors?'

'The son of an important friend. From long ago.'

Jose was intrigued. Adolfo teased him, often. 'But who *are* they, Tio?'

'You'll find out!'

'*Tio!*'

From the Posada, the road descended and passed the swimming pool which was reached by a criss-cross stone stairway. Adolfo paused at the parapet, took the pole from his shoulder and grinned at Jose. This was where they parted each morning – Adolfo moving down the stairway to the pool to take up his duties as attendant and Jose continuing to the whitewashed school building on the outskirts of Baucau. The pool was usually deserted this early in the day, but as Jose peered over the stonework he saw a man swimming, and on the far side lay a woman reading. He noticed she had white hair.

'There are our visitors, Tio. Tourist.'

'Yes,' his uncle said tensely. 'You'd better come and meet them.'

As they descended the stairway, Adolfo finally hissed from the side of his mouth: 'Big Red's son!'

Jose gasped. Big Red! Big Red, the Australian soldier. The name Jose had heard so many times in their conversations. Big Red, the fire-haired Australian fighter from across the seas. Adolfo had been his creado, his friend and helper during the war with the Japanese. It had been Adolfo who had always been at Big Red's side, carrying his gun, his food and his equipment. Most of the Australians had had their creados. But Jose knew that Big Red and Adolfo had become firm friends.

And now Big Red's son was here, in Baucau.

Since ever he could remember, Adolfo had whispered the stories to him, about the fighting, about the soldiers, about the man from overseas he had simply called 'Big Red'. Big Red the Australian soldier. The red-haired warrior!

As they came down the stairway, the man in the pool raised a hand out of the water. The woman too had seen them and got up from her chair. Jose noticed her hair wasn't really white but gold. It glistened in the morning light. She also wore large sunglasses and a big towel was draped around her body. Just as Jose reached the edge of the pool, the water turned into creamy blue foam as the man heaved himself out. Jose stepped back as if he'd been slapped. The man was so big! Huge. A large belly hung over the band of his bathing shorts like a sack of maize about to burst. He brushed the water from himself and held his hand out to Adolfo.

Jose's step faltered in surprise. He couldn't see a warrior, only a big man with a fat belly. He couldn't see a real warrior's son.

Water was still dripping from the man's face and shoulders as he pumped Adolfo's hand. 'You must be Adolfo, eh? You look just like my father said you would.' His face was split by a big grin. 'Even for the bamboo pole!' A warmth filled Jose's insides. He was suddenly glad of the trouble he had taken to learn English at Sister Philomena's class. He understood what the man was saying. Well, sort of.

A thick, wet arm encircled Adolfo's shoulders, soaking his shirt. Tio Adolfo seemed tiny, shrunken.

The man's voice was loud and echoed around the pool and into the trees beyond. 'Gee, it's good to meet you, Adolfo. My father talked about you so much!'

Adolfo ducked his head. 'I'm happy to meet with you,' he said in respectful, halting English. 'Happy, Senhor.'

'Jack, please. You must call me Jack.'

'Ah yes, Senhor Jack!'

They both laughed. Adolfo then put down the pole, carefully so he wouldn't damage the net. As he straightened up, the woman was beside him.

'Adolfo, at last,' she said in a soft voice, extending one hand, the other holding fast the edge of the large towel. Adolfo shook her hand gingerly, then turned to Jose. 'This is my sister Theresa's son, Jose.'

The woman smiled and said, 'Oh I'm very happy to meet you! Do you speak English?'

Jose nodded.

'Ah, I can see you're on your way to school.'

'Yes, Senhora!' She didn't speak English like Sister Philomena, but he understood her.

'Your bag seems to be full of books. Do you like school? Studying?'

'Yes, Senhora.'

'Do you know what you want to be when you leave school?' she said, lifting the sunglasses from her face. Her eyes were blue, blue like the sky.

'Yes, Senhora. I would like to be a lawyer, like my uncle in Lisboa.'

Adolfo touched his shoulder. 'You must go now, Jose, or you'll be late.'

Jose nodded. Reluctantly. He didn't want to go. He wanted to listen to them talking. He wanted to hear about the war, about Big Red. He wanted to hear the stories again, the stories Tio Adolfo had told so many times that he knew them off by heart.

He didn't look back as he made his way along the side of the pool and then across the grass to the stairway, and only when he had climbed the stairs to the top did he draw a big breath and put down his bag. He scrambled up on the parapet. Legs dangling over the side, he watched the three talk beside the pool. Senhor Jack and the Blonde Lady were seated at the table while Tio Adolfo stood beside them. Big Red. He could hardly believe it. 'Big Red's son, Senhor Jack,' he said out aloud. Big Red's name immediately brought visions before his eyes, men shooting at each other, Japanese and Australian soldiers, Adolfo and Big Red hiding in a tree trunk . . .

For a moment longer he sat and watched the three people below, then climbed down. I must hurry, he thought.

Then suddenly the gravel crackled behind him. He knew instantly who it would be. He turned. Bright red spots, as if painted, decorated Carmillo's puffed out cheeks. His white shirt was already wet with perspiration and clinging like transparent plastic to his fat shoulders. Luis and Franco were a step behind.

'Your uncle is telling lies again,' Carmillo said, a grin breaking on his chubby face. 'Telling lies to the tourists. About his Tree of Life that doesn't exist. All those war stories . . .'

'He's not telling lies . . .'

'He's always telling lies about the war . . .'

'No . . .!'

Jose made a dash for it. He started running up the gravelled road, conscious of his heavy school pack, but he had caught them by surprise and managed to put some distance between them. But he knew they would catch him: *they* weren't burdened by schoolbags. When he sensed them only a few steps behind, he whirled and tried to push his way between a startled Luis and Franco. Luis, again caught out, stumbled, then fell. It was Carmillo, however, because of his weight, who lumbered a good thirty metres behind, and had enough time to prepare. As Jose tried to pass, a fat heavy hand grabbed at his shirt and held tight.

'Ahhh!' Hot breath on his face.

'Not fast enough, eh?' the fat face said.

'Let me go, my uncle will come.'

'He's telling his lies. He's much too busy.'

The others were around him, pushing, pulling, jostling. They dragged him along the gravelled road until they were at the parapet. Jose struggled but Carmillo's arm was too strong. Suddenly Carmillo let go and Jose toppled backwards, the tiny frame of Luis stopping his fall. Franco, who was taller than Jose, and strong, twisted his arm.

Carmillo got up on the parapet and with hands on hips, an arrogant posture, he yelled down towards the pool. 'Hey, Adolfo! Tell us a story about the war! He-iii! Tell us another lie! Tell us about the Tree of Life!'

Jose tried to squirm out of Franco's hold. His arm hurt. He could see over the parapet but the three figures were too far away to hear Carmillo's shouts. Adolfo lifted his head and looked towards them once, and for a moment all three stared up at the parapet. But then they continued talking.

Angry that Adolfo didn't react, Carmillo turned on Jose. Clumsily he climbed down and with a face crimson with anger, jabbed a fat finger into Jose's chest. Jose winced with pain. 'Do you have any stories, Jose? Did Adolfo tell you any new stories about the war? Make-believe stories? He-ii! Tell us, tell?'

'They're true! All the stories are true. Adolfo doesn't lie!'

Carmillo moved closer, his nose almost touching Jose's. 'Lies, lies, all lies,' he screeched.

A punch hit Jose in the middle of his stomach and he

doubled over, the air knocked from his body. He wanted to vomit but then, slowly, as he coughed, air pumped back into his lungs. He straightened up and the others were already well down the road. Holding his belly, Jose slung his bag over his shoulder and started after them.

Although his belly hurt, he was angry and was going to take them on. But they had too much of a start. Just before Carmillo turned into the pathway which led to the school, he twisted sideways towards Jose and held up two fingers.

3

The Blonde Lady

'What was she like, Jose?' his mother asked. 'Did she have long hair, blonde like the other tourist ladies? Is it short? Is she pretty?'

Jose sat on the far side of the big kitchen table and pushed the rice and pork around the plate with his spoon. His head hung low as if he didn't want to take part in the conversation. He loved rice and pork but his mother seldom cooked it now. Pork had become too expensive.

'Well, speak Jose! What about you, Adolfo?' Theresa said irritably, busy with another bowl of food. She had come in late from the hospital and hadn't bothered to change from her nurse's uniform.

Adolfo sighed, as if the question irritated him. Miguel just continued eating, his eyes on the bowl before him.

Theresa asked again: 'Does she have blonde hair, Adolfo? Is it straight or curled? Well, answer me, Brother!'

'I don't know! Straight, I think.'

She turned to Jose. Angry. 'What is her hair like, Jose? Tell your Mamma.'

Jose couldn't recall the tourist lady's hair other than it was white, golden. And she wore sunglasses.

Theresa lost patience. 'Ahrrr,' she growled and slammed about with the plates.

Jose watched her. The pain was still there in his stomach. Whenever he moved his upper body too quickly, he felt like vomiting. He shuddered, remembering Carmillo's punch. He didn't want to be sick. The rice and pork were so good. So he ate slowly, savouring each mouthful.

'Are you going to see them again tomorrow, Adolfo?' Theresa continued.

Tio Adolfo nodded.

'Well, *when?*'

'They are coming to the pool.' He hesitated a moment, then said, 'They have something for me, something from Big Red, the Australian soldier. He died last year.'

Theresa was suddenly alert. 'Money? Are they going to give you money?'

'No, Senhor Jack said it was a medal.'

'Hmmph! You cannot eat medals.'

Miguel, Jose's stepfather, spoke for the first time. He wasn't home that often because he drove a truck for Old Wong between Baucau and Dili. And he never spoke much. He sat at the table, occasionally raising a bottle of beer to his lips. He always seemed to be drinking. 'The Portuguese will leave Timor soon,' he said, sucking noisily on the bottle.

Jose's ears pricked up. 'Father Petri said that the

Portuguese will soon leave Timor. It has become too expensive for them to stay.'

Both Adolfo and Miguel looked up from their bowls.

'He said that when they leave, the hot-heads will make trouble. He said the Indonesians could come too!'

'You know I don't like you talking like that,' Theresa said and turned towards the wood-heated stove. The kitchen was almost unbearably hot and tiny beads of perspiration stood out on her face. Jose noticed her cheeks and forehead glowed in the half-light from the single bulb above their heads.

Miguel shrugged. 'The Chinese only want Australian and American dollars from the tourist. Old Wong pays his suppliers in dollars. It's a sure sign.'

'Dollars?'

'The escudo will be worth nothing when they leave.'

Jose watched Adolfo carefully spoon small amounts of rice into his mouth. He wanted to talk to Adolfo about the medal and the cockfighting. 'Will Senhor Jack and the Blonde Lady come to the cockfights on Sunday?' He heard his mother's sharp intake of breath. Now she's really angry!

Adolfo shrugged without lifting his head. 'Probably!'

'All this rubbish about the cockfights!' Theresa slammed down a plate of fruit. 'There are more important things than the cockfights.'

Adolfo at last lifted his head. 'It's only talk.'

'Jose must get to his uncle Carlo in Lisboa before the Portuguese leave.' Theresa sucked in her breath. 'He must study hard. And all the talk I hear is about cockfighting. Unimportant talk. Idiots' talk!'

A tightness came into Jose's throat. They had discussed this before, and it upset him. 'Mamma, I don't want to go to my uncle Carlo in Lisboa. I want to stay here, with you and Adolfo and Miguel.'

'Your uncle Carlo will look after you.'

'But I don't *want* to!'

'Quiet!' Theresa said. 'Miguel and I agreed it would be best.'

But to Jose it all sounded so unreasonable. He hated his mother talking about Tio Carlo and Portugal. Lately, she talked of little else. He didn't want to study in Lisbon. He wanted only to stay in Baucau.

Adolfo tried to lead the conversation in another direction. 'Senhor Jack wants to drive to Balibo. He wants to hire the vehicle from the Posada. Rikki will have to drive it. He knows the way.'

'Why do they want to drive to Balibo?' Theresa asked.

'Senhor Jack said there were important oil maps, papers he had to get.' He placed the spoon carefully by the side of his plate and wiped his mouth with the back of his hand.

'Senhor Jack has oil business in Timor?' Jose asked. 'Do the oil people know about the bad times coming?'

Adolfo fell silent, as if an important thought had suddenly occurred to him.

Jose looked up, as did Miguel. Something overcame Adolfo.

'Tio?' Jose asked.

In a sudden jerk, Adolfo straightened his back and he lifted his head. His eyes glowed. 'My Tree of Life!' he said

25

softly, forming each word carefully. 'It will be a chance to see my Tree of Life! I will be able to visit it, see it, touch it!'

'In Balibo?' Jose queried. He knew the Tree of Life was at Bobonaro. Adolfo had told him about it, many times.

Theresa was angry again. 'All this nonsense about the Tree,' she said. 'That was all thirty years ago.'

'Senhor Jack wants to see it. I told him about it.'

'It's where Tio Adolfo hid with the Australian soldier. From the Japanese,' Jose added.

'I know the story. Backwards. It buzzes around like the sound of a bee.'

'It is because of the Tree, Sister, that we are here today,' Adolfo said solemnly.

Adolfo's face looked as if it had been carved from dark wood. Jose thought he had to say something. 'The Tree stands where Tio Adolfo fought the Japanese.'

'Tio Adolfo didn't fight anyone,' Theresa said in a whisper. 'He only carried food and ammunition. Like a pack pony.'

Adolfo ignored her. 'Senhor Jack wants to see the Tree. It is important. For both of us. Perhaps it is a last chance to see it.'

Theresa's eyes were wide, the whites luminous in the poor light. 'Last chance for *what*?'

Miguel burped.

'The Indonesians will come when the Portuguese leave!' Jose said.

'Our people will protect us,' Theresa said.

A belch shook Miguel's body. He coughed a laugh. '*Our people*? Fretilin? UDT? Apodeti? The others? There are so many of them. Each day there is a new party. They're already busy fighting each other. They will not protect the people. Only each other.'

At last the hot-heads had a name, Jose thought. 'Why do they have such names?' he asked his stepfather.

'Fretilin, UDT, Apodeti – ha, big names make them feel important.'

'The hot-heads?'

'It's all confusing,' Miguel said and took another large swallow of beer.

'But the Portuguese are still here. Is it safe to drive to Balibo?'

'Of course,' Adolfo said.

'Can I come?' asked Jose hopefully.

Tio Adolfo looked at him curiously. 'You want to come to Balibo?'

'I want to see the Tree of Life. More than anything, Tio!'

'Your place is in school, Jose,' Theresa said. 'You must study.'

'Mamma, please!'

She turned her head away, busy on the stove.

'Mamma, *please*?'

Tio Adolfo rose. 'I will mention it to Senhor Jack tomorrow.'

Later, Jose went out onto the veranda with Tio Adolfo while his mother and Miguel sat around the kitchen table. His mother and Miguel talked a lot lately. Their conversation was a hissed whisper.

The veranda of the split-palm house was the coolest

place in the evening, for the inside hadn't had time to expel the heat of the day. Sitting on the steps near the front door, Jose noticed a breath of a breeze from the Mata Bien mountain range which usually offered a small measure of relief. Adolfo sat with his back to the veranda post and slowly rolled himself a thick cigarette from clove-spiced tobacco and a tear of newspaper.

Jose loved this part of the evening, talking with Tio Adolfo. Miguel never talked to him, not like Adolfo did. Miguel was only interested in talking about trucks and the soccer news from Portugal. But with Adolfo it was different. Jose's heart filled with warmth as he watched the flare of the match. There was always a sadness about Tio Adolfo, and though he tried to inject occasional humour into bits of his conversation, his laughter seemed forced and embarrassingly grotesque.

'Be gentle with your uncle,' his mother once told him. 'Tio Adolfo has had a hard life and has suffered a lot.' It was as if Tio Adolfo was possessed by a spirit which made him sad, but Jose knew it was not like that at all. Jose loved Adolfo, a love that was only matched by that he had for his mother.

In a way, Jose knew what bothered his uncle. Or at least he thought he did. Adolfo had been a creado to Senhor Red, but now he cleaned the pool for the officers and tourists and lost badly on the cockfights. Jose understood how Adolfo felt sadness in his heart. But he also knew of Adolfo's strength and courage. Especially his courage. It was something which made Jose strong too.

As the flame from the match died and Adolfo's face

disappeared in the dim light, as if by magic the pain Jose had felt earlier in the night from Carmillo's blow left his belly. 'Will you bet on the birds this Sunday, Tio?'

'Of course!' The cigarette flared again in a bright glow. 'But all the birds belong to Rikki so it really doesn't matter.'

Adolfo became silent.

'Then why do you bet, Tio?'

'I bet to win, Jose.'

'But you don't win often.'

'I will again.' After a moment, he asked: 'Was that Carmillo up on the road this morning?'

'Yes.'

There was a long pause. 'He will become like his father. His heart will become bitter.'

'Why does Rikki hate you so much?'

Adolfo sighed. 'It goes back, oh, a long time. His father was a bad man, a criminal who was sent to Timor. He hated his own people. He wanted to return to Portugal but the police didn't let him. That's why he *hated* so much. And Rikki took over his father's hate of the Portuguese. He thinks they are responsible for his father's bitterness. He wants the Indonesians to come and chase out the Portuguese. He thinks they will make him a big man, a Chef de Posto, give him an official post. He thinks he will become a Very Important Person.'

'But why does he hate *you*?'

'During the war I helped the Australians. His father's hate for the Portuguese became his own hate for the Portuguese and he thought the Japanese would drive them from Timor.'

'He helped the Japanese?'

'Yes. Then the Japanese left and Timor is still Portuguese.'

'But you place your money with Rikki!'

'There is no other way.'

Jose thought for a while. 'Why don't we buy our own fighting cock, Tio?'

A sharp laugh split the night. 'It would be a joke! Rikki's birds are the finest. Besides, it costs too much.'

Jose understood. Money existed as occasional pocket-money, but escudos were used to buy food and other items at Old Wong's store. He understood it was hard to earn a lot of money.

They sat in the almost-dark a long time, not speaking. Then Adolfo whispered: 'You must go to bed now. It is late.'

'Let's talk about the cockfights a little longer.'

'I don't want to talk about the fights. I have to think about Senhor Jack and the Lady.'

'What about the medal they said they brought with them. When will they give it to you?'

'Tomorrow.'

'Why didn't you get a medal before?'

Tio Adolfo sighed. 'The creados didn't get medals, Jose. Portugal was not at war with the Japanese. A few of the Portuguese men were honoured. But only a few. Not the Timorese. It was the Australian soldiers who came back after the war who honoured us. Not the Portuguese government.'

'You will be honoured tomorrow, Tio?'

'No, it is a personal thing. The medal belonged to Senhor Big Red.'

Jose's heart thumped powerfully. 'It is a gift, a gift of honour.'

'I suppose it is.'

'Does it have to do with the hollow tree trunk where you and Senhor Big Red hid from the Japanese? The Tree of Life?'

Adolfo didn't answer.

'Tell me about the war. About the hollow trunk on the way to Bobonaro?'

'Not tonight.' For a second, Jose saw his uncle's craggy face light up as he pulled on the cigarette. 'Not tonight.'

Electricity for their house was supplied by a generator at the hospital where Theresa worked. But Miguel was suspicious of electricity. He said the light at night was too powerful and damaged the eyes. After the evening meal, he usually switched off the main power, and kerosene lamps were lit. Jose knew it had nothing to do with eye damage, but about saving money.

There was a lamp on a low table beside Jose's bed. The big square wick held a strong flame contained in a bulb-shaped glass, open at the top. The rim was dark with soot. Its light was soft and yellow and only strong enough to illuminate the immediate area around his bed; there were gloomy shadows on the walls and ceilings.

Under the top of the bedside table was a shelf where Jose stored his cigar box. A present from Tio Tschia in Dili. The box contained his dearest possessions – a gold coin, a silver Confirmation medal with the red ribbon still attached, a few old coins, a ballpoint pen, a couple of glass marbles and a magnifying glass with a silver handle. There was also a black-and-white framed photograph of a man in an officer's uniform. His Portuguese father.

Tio Adolfo had given him the glass frame, bought at Old Wong's store, because the photograph had already got frayed edges, and was ripped in a couple of places by too much handling. Jose held the image up to the light and studied it carefully. The insignia on the cap. The markings on the shoulders. The clean-shaven round jaw. The eyes dark and focused somewhere to the side. He looked at the photograph often. Sometimes it made him happy to see it: it made him feel as though his father was near him, giving strength. Other times, it made him feel sad and alone.

There was sand in his eyes, and several times Jose rubbed hard to relieve the itch. He put the photograph back in the box and stored it carefully. He wanted desperately to sleep now but the burning under his eyelids kept him awake.

Suddenly his mother was beside him. Jose felt her hand on his brow, soft, warm, loving. 'Mamma?'

'Ssssh! Don't talk. Sleep!'

The hand kept stroking his forehead. The itching had stopped.

'Miguel and I have talked a lot over the last week,' he heard her whisper. 'The troubles are coming. There will be fighting; it will be dangerous for you, for us all. You know you must go to Uncle Carlo in Lisboa. He and his family will look after you. You will study there . . .'

Slipping in and out of sleep, he said: 'I don't want to leave, Mamma!' Sudden panic startled him awake. 'No, I don't want to.'

Her hand soothed him back. 'You will never leave *me*, Jose. You will only be away for a little while. To study and become someone.'

'Yes, Mamma.' It suddenly came to him: 'The woman had soft-soft hair, soft like yours!'

'Oh Jose!' Lips brushed his brow.

Her voice floated above him, somewhere, and then he was asleep.

4

Theresa Asks for Help

Jose had never seen Sister Philomena so agitated. She sighed constantly, sucked in her breath, then noisily puffed her cheeks as she stood in front of the class. She was fanning her wet, shining black face with a sheaf of paper. 'I must go to Dili,' she announced dramatically and dismissed the class for the day. As they shuffled out into the morning heat, Carmillo had the answer right away. 'It's the troubles,' he whispered. A thick arm came around Jose's shoulders and fingers squeezed above the elbow. 'She's going to see the Bishop!'

'Ouch! That hurts.'

Carmillo removed his arm. 'It's the Bishop she's seeing.'

'How would *you* know?'

'My father told me last night she would go!'

As Jose made his way along the gravelled road, the Posada Land Rover went past in a cloud of dust. Carmillo's father, Rikki, was at the wheel with Sister Philomena beside him, still fanning her face.

The troubles were serious enough for Rikki to drive Sister Philomena to Dili to see the Bishop, serious enough to close the school for the day.

At the pool, Adolfo was cleaning out leaves and insects with his net.

'Did you get the medal, Tio? The medal they promised you?'

Adolfo shook his head without interrupting the flow of his work. 'I saw the medal, I held it in my hand,' he said slowly. 'It was gold and shiny, with a red ribbon.' He sighed. 'But it is Senhor Red's medal and not mine.'

'You never got a medal! You should have got one!'

'My own medal, not a medal that belonged to someone else. It's not right.' Then he added, 'Senhor Jack understood and we will talk about it no more.'

Jose followed his uncle around the pool. After a while, Adolfo said, 'I don't need a medal for the fighting, Jose. It was enough to see Senhor Red again when he returned with the other soldiers after the war. He said he would come back to us and he did. That was enough.'

'Where are Senhor Jack and the Blonde Lady now?'

'They've gone to eat at Old Wong's shop.'

'Will they come back, here, to the pool?'

'I'm sure,' Adolfo smiled. 'They are the only tourists at the Posada.' He grunted as he pulled a large dead moth out of the water.

'Tourists are afraid to come to Timor,' Jose said to himself.

He became bored watching his uncle work the pool. It was also very hot so he made himself comfortable in the shade of the palm tree and thought about what Adolfo had said. He was soon asleep.

Voices close by. Senhor Jack talking to Adolfo on the side of the pool. Jose jumped up and rubbed his eyes. The Blonde Lady was sitting in the shade of the palm, a book in her hand.

She smiled when she saw Jose. 'I nearly fell asleep myself. I heard you got the day off from school.'

'Yes, Senhora!'

'A surprise holiday, eh?'

'Sister Philomena had to drive to Dili to see the Bishop.'

'The Bishop? That sounds important.'

'It's because of the troubles, Senhora. Carmillo said so.'

'Carmillo. Is he your friend?'

Jose hesitated a moment, then said, 'He punches me a lot.'

'Ah,' the Blonde Lady seemed amused. 'The school bully. Everyone has them.' She smiled. 'You know in Australia I teach at a school which has only girls. Is there such a school in Timor?'

'Yes, Senhora.'

'We live in Sydney. Have you ever heard of Sydney?'

Jose wasn't sure. He'd heard of Darwin, only an hour's flight from Dili on the Australian plane. Darwin, where they made the lemonade you could buy at Old Wong's store; and of course Tia Amelia in Dili always had a bottle for him. He'd also heard of Broome where they fished for pearls. But Sydney? He shook his head.

'Sydney is a very big city with many people. And there is a beautiful harbour.'

'Like Dili?'

'But much, much bigger. And many millions of people live around the harbour. Do you think you might want to see Sydney one day?'

'Oh yes!' He would also like to see Lisbon and New York. A tourist at the pool once had told him about New York.

The Blonde Lady thought for a moment, then said in a different voice: 'Your mother is a very strong, determined lady.' She placed her book on the grass. 'She came to talk with us when we had lunch at the Chinese shop. It takes determination to do that. And desperation. She really wants you out of Timor before things get worse.' She paused a moment. 'Jack and I promised to do all we can to help get you to your father's people in Portugal. This place is going to explode real soon, that's for sure.'

'My mother speaks *English*?' He couldn't believe it! She had never let on.

The Blonde Lady laughed. 'And very good English too! She told me she learned when she did her nursing training.'

'Learnt *English*?'

She laughed again. 'Never underestimate your mother.'

Jose was suddenly fearful. 'Will you take me to Lisboa to Uncle Carlo and my grandmother?'

'Now hold on, not so fast. You just can't leave Timor from one day to the next. You've got to get visas, a passport, documents, and money most of all. I told you, Jack and I promised Adolfo and your mother we will do all we can. But you've got to be patient.'

That night in bed as he studied his father's photograph, Jose's jaw trembled and he felt terribly, terribly alone. The conversation with the Blonde Lady had upset him. His mother wanted him to go to Tio Carlo and study in Lisbon. He didn't want that. He just wanted to continue going to school, to the cockfights with Adolfo on Sunday, to be near his mother. He didn't want to leave Timor.

He reached over to the small table and propped the photograph up against the cigar box and angled it so that the yellow light from the lamp fell on it from the side. Papa, you will know what I should do! 'Papa? Papa?' he whispered. 'Please help me, Papa, please?'

Tears ran down his cheeks and soon, exhausted, he fell asleep. In the morning the photograph was still propped up against the cigar box, though someone had turned off the lamp. He remembered he'd had a dream, a dream about a fighting cock with feathers the colour of the rainbow. It had been his own bird, and he had matched it against one of Carmillo's white cocks. His own bird had won and he had carried it out of the pit in triumph.

It was a strange dream and it haunted him for the rest of the day.

5

The Chef de Posto

Sister Philomena talked about oil in Timor. She said that the people around Suai on the south coast used the black mud from the nearby swamps to light their lamps. Engineers were now drilling for oil, both on land and sea, and if it was found in great quantity it would mean prosperity for Timor. Luis was stood in front of the class to hold up a shiny poster showing a drilling platform built on concrete and steel pylons over the water, and Sister Philomena explained that men lived on them for months at a time.

Senhor Jack was an engineer with the Australian oil company. Jose wondered if he and the Blonde Lady lived on a platform over the sea.

Carmillo put his hand up to ask a question: 'How do the men wash their clothes if they have no women on the platforms?'

Sister Philomena said the platform had special teams of men who washed clothes for everyone.

'Men washing clothes for men?'

A burst of laughter. Sister Philomena cracked a stick down on her desk.

Jose laughed with the rest. How men could wash clothes for other men!

Later in the morning, Carmillo turned to Jose while Sister Philomena was busy at the rear of the room. 'Gomez is gone!' he whispered.

'Where?'

'Gone!'

He liked Gomez dos Santos. They often spent time together, playing football or helping each other with schoolwork. Perhaps he was ill. Sister Philomena would know.

When Gomez hadn't arrived by the morning recess Jose decided to ask. As the others made for the door, Jose pushed his head down under the desk and pretended to look for a book in his bag. He wanted to be last out. Carmillo, on the other side of the desk, eyed him suspiciously. As Jose tried to straighten up, Carmillo shoved him hard. Jose's hip connected with the edge of the desk. He winced in pain.

It was as if Carmillo knew why Jose wanted to talk to Sister Philomena. 'Gomez is a coward,' he said, 'just like the others!'

'He's not!'

'My father said pigeons always fly when the hunter approaches.'

Sister Philomena, her black shiny face distorted in anger, yelled from the door. 'Carmillo, Jose, out, now!'

With Carmillo in the lead, they hurried along the line of desks. As they ducked through the door, Sister Philomena clipped each on the side of the head with the flat of her hand.

At lunchtime, they played soccer in the side area between the school building and the barracks. As Sister Philomena came past Jose, she placed a hand on his shoulder. He thought she might still be angry but she wasn't. 'Gomez won't be coming back, Jose.' She spoke a curious Portuguese. She came from Angola and Jose sometimes had trouble understanding. But now she just sighed and she didn't smile as she usually did. Sister Philomena always smiled.

'The family left for Portugal on the weekend – the third this week,' she said.

Jose was surprised to find his mother standing at the school gate. Instead of the white nurse's uniform she wore during the day, she had on a dark blue blouse and a grey skirt. Around her throat was the necklace with the red stones she said his father had given her just before his death – his death in a military vehicle in the mountains. The necklace came from Portugal, his mother had said, a long time ago. She only dresses like that on Sundays, Jose thought.

'We've an appointment to see the Chef de Posto,' she said, taking his hand. 'He's waiting for us!'

Theresa had a strong, purposeful walk. She always breathed heavily when there was a task to be done. Several times the strap of Jose's schoolbag slipped off his shoulder and he had to stop and readjust it. She hissed irritably. By the time they passed the ruins of the market building and walked up the gentle incline towards the pool, Jose was puffing and sweat trickled down his spine.

'We'll stop here a moment,' his mother said. She sat on the parapet and waved a white handkerchief about to cool her face. Jose peered over the edge and saw Adolfo below, working the pole around the edge of the pool. He didn't dare shout a greeting, but as if Adolfo knew he would be there, he lifted his head, then smiled and raised a hand.

Theresa ignored her brother and pulled at Jose's arm. 'Come, we'd better go. I don't want to be late.'

A few minutes later they sat in the corridor of the main administrative building. There were many people waiting, all of them Chinese, sitting tightly pressed together on wooden benches, and all of them neat in suits and white shirts. Many wore ties. An army officer Jose recognised from the pool peered over the top of his clipboard and winked at him. Jose smiled back. The officer read out names. One by one, the Chinese disappeared through the door at the far end of the corridor.

'Will we have to wait long?' Jose whispered.

'Hush!' Theresa wiped her face with the white handkerchief.

After a long time: 'Rodrigus, Theresa,' the officer said in a loud voice.

'Come!' And she grabbed Jose's hand so hard he nearly dropped his schoolbag. They followed the officer down the corridor. Just as they were about to enter the room, Theresa turned and looked down at Jose. Her tongue clicked. She licked her fingers and with her wet thumb, brushed his hair away from his eyes.

The Chef de Posto was a familiar figure around Baucau. Weeks before he had addressed the school in the assembly yard and told them that Timor would always be part of Portugal. He was a huge man with a curved beak of a nose and silvery hair and he was seldom without a pipe clamped in a corner of his mouth. As they came into the room, he said a soft 'Ah!' and then he rose from behind the cluttered desk and his chair snapped back with a loud crack. He held the pipe in his left hand, the other extended to take Theresa's. Jose peered up at the man.

'Ah, Senhora Rodrigus, Bon Dia! It's good to see you!' He waved the pipe before his eyes and indicated a chair by the desk. Jose remained standing beside his mother. The Chef de Posto's eyes suddenly focused on him. 'And how you've grown, Jose. Eh? A young man, and handsome, just like your father.'

The chair creaked again. Sparks and ashes flew out of the pipe. A blue-grey cloud formed over the man's white hair. 'Your father and I were in Angola together, fighting for Portugal, you know? For two years! Then we were posted to Timor. Ah, we were together a lot, brother warriors!'

Jose nodded.

The pipe moved before the man's face, throwing off more smoke. 'Well, that was a long time ago.' He sucked on the pipe but it had gone out. A match flared. The pipe made a bit of noise. 'So you want to study in Portugal, eh? What are you going to study? Law? Medicine, become a doctor to make people well? Eh? An engineer? Always a good profession for a boy. No? Perhaps you'd like to join the army, be an officer like your father, eh?'

'A lawyer, Senhor, like my uncle Carlo,' Jose answered.

'A lawyer, eh?'

Using his right thumb and forefinger, the man began stuffing tobacco into his pipe. He didn't look up when he said: 'Now Senhora, about your application...' He pushed the stem into his mouth and while he held a match over the bowl, he sucked noisily. 'It helps, you know, if the child has relatives in Portugal, and of course he's the son of an officer...'

The voices merged into the background. Jose noticed the gold markings on the Chef de Posto's collar and those on a panel on his shoulders. His mother wanted him to become somebody like that.

He looked about the room. He was conscious of words as they floated about. The troubles. Australia. Lisbon. Visas. Money...

Then suddenly the Chef de Posto's voice boomed in his ear. The man was beside him, a giant figure. Jose lifted his head but all he saw was the man's trousers and belt. A heavy, strong hand clamped down on his shoulder.

'Come, Jose, see this photo?' He stabbed at a black-and-white image with the stem of his pipe. 'That's your father and me. In Lisboa on our return from Angola.'

Jose stood on tiptoe trying to see more of his father. Both men were in uniform, smiling at the camera. He didn't recognise either of them. The photo certainly wasn't like the one he had in his bedroom. These men were just smiling soldiers.

But the soldiers are all tired of fighting, Jose thought. Father Petri had said that. They are tired of war, of fighting on foreign soil. But what was Timor? Didn't the Chef de Posto say only a few weeks ago that Timor would always remain part of Portugal?

A hand smashed down on his back so hard that Jose jumped. Then there were loud voices, noise, and the faces of Chinese looming out of a fog as he and his mother pushed their way through the people in the corridor. At last they were out in the hot, late afternoon sun, walking up the gravelled road.

'There's a chance, a very good chance,' his mother said, more to herself than Jose.

'A chance?'

Theresa stopped and blinked down at him. 'For you to study in Portugal,' she said.

Jose's heart thumped. *I don't want to study in Portugal. They don't have cockfights in Portugal. I don't want to leave you, Mamma! I don't want to leave Adolfo.*

'I don't want to leave,' he said aloud. His throat felt very dry.

'I know you don't, but it's best.' She touched his cheek with a finger, bit her lip, grabbed his elbow and pulled him along the gravelled road.

When they reached the parapet above the pool, Theresa said she had to return to the hospital. 'Go down and see your uncle,' she added, and moved off.

But there was no sign of Adolfo below. Jose thought he might be at the small house at the rear where they kept the machine that cleaned the pool. But he had no time to look – suddenly, Carmillo and Luis were at his side. Jose tried to get between them but Carmillo's bulky body pushed against him.

'You've been to see the Chef de Posto!' Carmillo said, his cheeks red as carrots. 'The cowards are fleeing Timor. My father was right. The hunters are approaching, and the cowards are looking to hide!'

'We're not leaving,' Jose said, stubbornly. 'I'm not going to Lisboa.'

'Ah, so it's Lisboa, eh?'

'No!'

'Coward, you're a coward who's fleeing. Like Gomez and the others.'

'I'm not a coward.'

'Coward!' Carmillo continued and pushed against Jose's chest with both his hands. Jose fell against the rough concrete of the parapet. The edge of it felt as if someone had lashed him with a stick, horizontally across the small of his back. 'Coward!' Carmillo hissed again and was ready to push him once more. But he was slow to move, and there was a gap between Carmillo's huge body and Luis. Jose saw his chance. He ducked his head and swiftly moved between them. He was vaguely aware of Carmillo turning but it was too late. Jose was on the gravelled road and running, running, running. Even with his schoolbag, he knew he could outrun Carmillo. Easily.

'Coward, coward!' he heard Carmillo yell. The voice faded quickly as he ran up the gravelled road.

6

Adolfo and the War

Jose saw Adolfo's face change when he talked about the war. His eyes danced about in their sockets and it was as if a thin mist hid his vision; he saw only what was inside his head. He didn't see Jose sitting opposite him on the veranda steps. What he remembered was happening before his eyes. 'I carried the ammunition, food and water, and occasionally Senhor Red would allow me to put the rifle on my back,' he said, drawing on his thick cigarette. The tobacco spiced with cloves gave off a heady aroma.

'Why do you call him Senhor Red?' Jose knew why but he wanted to hear yet again.

'His hair was the colour of fire. It glowed in the sun.'

'Tell me about the Tree of Life.' He had heard the story countless times.

'You know the story.'

'I want to hear it again.'

Tio Adolfo sighed, like he didn't want to speak. But

once he started, the words came evenly and smoothly, as if he was reciting. 'The Japanese chased us right up past Bobonaro where they were building a road. We were running towards some trees and then we knew it was a trap. The Japanese were in the trees and firing at us. One of the Australians was killed, also two of the creados. One was from my village. From Ermera. The men were blowing the hoholo from the hills to warn us. We could hear the horn very clearly and knew that the Japanese had trapped us.'

'Were there many Japanese?'

'Many. The crack of their guns was very near. And we heard the bullets whistling past, pweeeee, pweeee, just like that. Senhor Red and I ran across to another line of trees and there we found a large burnt-out stump. We crawled into it through a hole an animal had made and then pulled some burnt pieces of timber across it. It was almost like a tiny room. We could even stand up in it.'

Jose sucked in his breath. The story still excited.

'We stood in the trunk two days and nights and the Japanese came past us many times. We could hear shots and shouting and once we heard the voices of creados they had captured. They were shot not far from the Tree – we could hear them. When we finally crawled out of the Tree, the Japanese had gone.'

Adolfo paused and pulled on the cigarette one more time before throwing it into the dark. After a while he said: 'It was soon after that that Senhor Red fell into the fire. He burnt his arm badly. The medical man put a white bandage on it but the officer said that he would have to leave us. We all went down the coast the next night and the submarine did come, just like the officer said it would. They paddled out to it in a rubber boat!'

He shook his head as if he couldn't quite believe his own memory. 'The officer talked with the underwater boat by radio and it sent a small rubber boat out. Senhor Red didn't take his gun but gave it to one of the other men. He took my hand in his and promised to come back. Afterwards, after the war. He said we would get drunk together.'

'And he did come back!' Jose whispered.

'He did. And we did get drunk, behind Old Wong's store, on beer. Senhor Red came twice more to visit us, the last time with many of the other soldiers. There were celebrations in Dili with our people. There was marching and a military band made a lot of noise . . .'

'Did you march, Tio?'

'No, I didn't march. But I shook the hand of the chief of soldiers from Australia. Later, there was a big banquet at the barracks with our Portuguese officers and men and the Australian chief wanted me to tell him about the Tree of Life.'

'You told him?'

'He said it was a remarkable escape.'

But something still puzzled Jose. 'Why do people make fun of you? Yelling that you tell stories, made-up stories. Why does Carmillo's father say you lie?'

'Rikki must have something to hate.'

'I don't understand.'

'It makes him feel better to have reason to hate. It makes him feel important.'

'But the Tree exists, doesn't it?'

'It exists and we will see it soon. Rikki will see it, too. He will drive the vehicle from the Posada.'

'Rikki?' Jose said in surprise.

'He knows the way and can take care of the vehicle if there are problems with the engine. Besides, it is his job to drive tourists around Timor.'

'Senhor Jack and the Blonde Lady will see the Tree, too?'

'Yes.'

'Perhaps they can take a photograph of it and I can show it at school?'

'It's not that important. It is more important that Senhor Jack gets all his oil maps and reports.'

Jose was suddenly alert. So that was the real reason for driving to Balibo. 'Are they secret maps and reports?' he asked in a low voice.

Adolfo laughed. 'They are only papers Senhor Jack must have. They are important to the oil company. The charts and reports are the result of many years of work. Senhor Jack does not want them to fall into other people's hands.'

'The hot-heads?'

'The papers belong to the oil people. No one else.'

Jose sensed his uncle tense.

Adolfo waved a hand. 'The Tree of Life. Senhor Jack wants to see it. It is also important to him. I will show him. How Senhor Red and I hid in the trunk. And Senhor Jack and the Blonde Lady want *you* to come, too.'

Jose swallowed hard. 'But what about Mamma? And Sister Philomena?'

'It is all arranged.'

7

Lemonade

Jose and Adolfo walked along the gravelled road towards the tourist Posada in the half light of dawn. The four-wheel-drive vehicle was parked in front, and Rikki was already busy cleaning the side windows.

'Aee-ie!' he shouted when he saw them coming, flapping a piece of rag. 'There are no pools to clean in Balibo!'

'He's evil,' Adolfo said almost in a whisper.

'Aeii, and you've brought your professor. Hey, professor? What will you learn in Balibo?'

'More than you!' retorted Jose.

'Aee-ie! A spirited one, too!'

'Leave the boy,' Adolfo growled. 'He has no part in your evil cruelty.'

Just then, Senhor Jack and the Blonde Lady came down the steps of the inn, with Toni carrying their bags a few steps behind.

'Bon Dio!' Senhor Jack said and grinned. 'Bon *Dia*!'

Adolfo kicked up his heels. 'Ah, Bon Dia, Senhor Jack. You are learning Portuguese.'

Senhor Jack laughed lightly. 'I do want to get beyond the "Good Morning" stage.'

When Toni placed the bags in the back of the vehicle, Senhor Jack pulled himself up into the front passenger seat, with Jose and the Blonde Lady in the rear. Adolfo squatted in the back among the spare tyres, the big tool box and a basket of sandwiches and fresh fruit.

'All right, let's go, let's go!' Senhor Jack shouted.

Rikki bounced into the driver's seat and with a dramatic gesture, pulled on stained pig-skin gloves, and through the open window he adjusted the rear-vision mirror. 'A few hours to Dili,' Rikki said in Tetum.

'What's he saying? What's he talking about?' Senhor Jack yelled over the whine of the motor. Rikki didn't speak English so Adolfo had to shout his translation from the back.

'He's talking about Dili, Senhor!'

Senhor Jack threw up his hands. 'Adolfo, you'd better sit with Judy. Otherwise we'll shout ourselves hoarse. Stop the vehicle and you can change places!' he yelled.

As the Land Rover lurched to a halt, Adolfo got out and swapped seats with Jose. First he made sure Jose was comfortable. By pushing the bags to one side, and folding two thick blankets under him, Jose had a soft seat.

'Sure you'll be all right in the back there?' the Blonde Lady asked. She seemed very concerned. Several times she twisted her head to take a quick look at how Adolfo had arranged things. 'If the bags bother you, tell me.'

'Yes, Senhora.'

'All right.'

Outside, Toni the gardener stood waving on the steps of the Posada. Ezra, the Posada cook, suddenly appeared beside him, still wearing his white apron. He too raised his hand in farewell.

A few hours later they were on the outskirts of Dili. The Blonde Lady was uncomfortable and the handkerchief she kept wiping over her face was wet. Every time the vehicle lurched over a pothole or rattled over a corrugated section of the roadway, she moaned softly. Occasionally Senhor Jack would turn in the passenger seat and ask if she was all right.

'Adolfo said Dili is up ahead,' Senhor Jack reassured.

'Thank God,' the Blonde Lady sighed.

'Tia Amelia will be happy to see you!' Adolfo said to Jose. Jose loved his Tia Amelia, his mother's older sister. When Rikki parked the vehicle in front of the Hotel Mimosa, where Senhor Jack and the Blonde Lady were to have lunch and stay the night, the walk to Tia Amelia's was only short. Her husband, Tio Tschia, owned one of the big trading houses in the capital. Rikki was to remain with the vehicle and after his lunch was to fill it with petrol from the pump at the military barracks.

With Adolfo leading, they made their way through the broad streets of Dili. Jose gradually fell behind his uncle as he stared at the many people, the large houses, the motorcycles roaring past. Several army trucks crammed with young Portuguese soldiers threw up clouds of dust. The soldiers were singing.

Adolfo stopped in front of the long, white-washed administration building, grand with its arches. 'Come, we'd better keep going. They'll be waiting for us,' Adolfo said.

'Just let me look a moment longer!' Jose glanced back at some soldiers, standing on either side of the doorway. He had never seen soldiers like that in Baucau. They were Timorese, mountain men, with headdresses made from colourful feathers bright in the sun, their chests bare and glistening. They had on knee-high army boots and held heavy, broad-bladed machetes crossed over their thighs.

To get to Tia Amelia's they had to go through the main store. Over the doorway big letters spelled out 'Canton Trading Company' in Portuguese. Tio Tschia had named his business in honour of the town in China where he was born. All at once, the aroma from his previous visits came back to Jose. Deliciously sweet curry that made him sneeze, coffee, cloves, a hundred spices, foods, drinks, tools in one corner, machinery in another. And Tio Tschia, a tall Chinese dressed in a batik shirt, the fabric stretching over his enormous stomach, stood behind the counter and beamed a welcome.

'Ah, Adolfo and Jose! Bon Dia, Bon Dia!' he said in Portuguese. He shook Adolfo's hand, then Jose's. His grip was soft and warm. 'You've grown, ah yes, how you've grown. You'll be a man soon, eh?'

'Yii-eh! How you've grown,' Tia Amelia repeated, rolling her eyes. She pulled Jose hard against her ample waist. His nostrils were filled with spices and sweat. 'Oh yes, how you've grown.'

Lunch was already on the table. Although his grandpa and his grandmother had been Portuguese – that is, Grandmother had a Portuguese father and Timorese mother – Jose had been accustomed to Cantonese cooking since he could walk. He loved Tia Amelia's food: pork pieces flavoured with plum and soya bean sauces, the crunchy chicken, the fried rice and, most of all, the big bottle of lemonade from Australia. Tia Amelia had an electric icebox and the lemonade was cold when he touched the bottle, and wet and frosty with condensed moisture. Jose sometimes bought a Coca Cola, or cans of soft drink at Old Wong's store, but this was best. He downed the first glass almost in one gulp.

'Not so fast, slowly, slowly,' his aunt warned.

Jose studied the colourful label. It was in English and he recognised a few words. One of them was 'Darwin'. He knew that Darwin was a town across the waters. All the tourists flew in from Darwin.

Uncle Tschia sat with them while they ate and spoke about the troubles in a slow, deliberate way.

'You should go, leave,' Adolfo said solemnly. He leaned back and started to roll himself a cigarette. 'You have too much to lose. If the Indonesians come, the Chinese people will have many problems.'

'Why the Chinese people, Tio?' asked Jose, pouring himself another lemonade.

'The Chinese are the traders, the people who run the stores in Timor, Jose. Many people are jealous.'

'The hot-heads again?'

'Those people who are jealous.'

'The Indonesians then?'

Tio Tschia was breathing heavily. 'They will not come, Adolfo.'

Adolfo shook his head, and Jose got the impression his uncles didn't care to talk about the troubles any more.

In the afternoon, Tio Tschia and Tia Amelia walked with Jose down to the waterfront. Many other people seemed to be walking in the same direction. They walked along the path on the foreshore and Tio Tschia pointed out the rusty hulks of ships still lying about. 'These were landing craft from the last war, weren't they?' Jose asked, and shrugged. 'They will be there until they rot.'

Then, from the pier behind the long warehouse, Jose saw the big grey-painted Portuguese ship. It had already drawn away from the wharf and now, as it turned to head out into Dili Bay, it moved into position side-on to the crowd. There was a loud rumble from the ship's engine and the water boiled at the stern, then another loud noise and all movement ceased. Tio Tschia had his arm over Jose's shoulder and on his other side Tia Amelia pressed a handkerchief to her eyes. 'It's so sad, so sad,' she mumbled. 'They were good boys.'

'Why are they leaving, Tio?' Jose asked.

'They are going home.' He shook his head.

'Tio Adolfo said that.'

'It is the truth.'

The soldiers onboard ship had now lined up at the railing, two deep, their faces turned shorewards. People spilled from the wharf onto the soft sand of Dili beach.

Jose wanted to move down too, but Tio Tschia held him back. 'This is the best position here.'

Jose saw the soldiers clearly across the short distance. Their hands were behind their backs and their shirts stretched tight over chests and shoulders. Suddenly, a loud, sharp command echoed over Dili Bay and the soldiers' throats burst in a melodious, beautiful song. Jose saw how the soldiers strained to sing, their mouths wide, their heads high. It made his skin prickle. Loud sobs shook Tia Amelia. Tio Tschia's arm became heavier.

The soldiers sang a number of songs, and just as dramatically as they had begun, they abruptly stopped. For a few moments, the only sound over the water was the soft throb of the ship's engine. Then, the soldiers broke their line and mobbed to the rails, cheering madly. The crowd too erupted, frantically flapping hands, scarves, pieces of cloth towards the ship. Caught up in it all, Jose too shouted his words of farewell across the water. 'Goodbye! Goodbye!' and his words merged with those from the crowd.

It boiled again around the ship. Then the ship turned and slowly began to nose its way across Dili Bay. The soldiers began to sing again and the people listened in silence. Finally, the ship was only a shadowy shape out in the Bay and the sound of singing was a faint sound, like a distant echo.

Tia Amelia gave Jose one of her smothering hugs and as they walked through the store, Tio Tschia flapped his hands for Jose to come with him behind the counter. 'This is for you, Jose,' he said and winked. He thrust a brown paper bag into his hands, then pinched his cheek and winked again. Once out in the street, Jose opened the bag and his face split into a wide grin when he saw the colourfully wrapped cubes of chewing gum. The soldiers at the barracks in Baucau chewed gum. Now he too had some!

8

The Tree of Life

They left the low coastal plain and as soon as the outskirts of Dili were cleared, the Land Rover began to climb steadily, its low gear grating and whining. Senhor Jack was very enthusiastic about everything, asking Adolfo one question after another. The Blonde Lady too seemed more comfortable than she had been on the Baucau-Dili stretch and talked more to her husband. Several times she asked Adolfo to translate what Rikki was grumbling about.

'He says he's still hungry. He's looking forward to his evening meal.'

The Blonde Lady laughed. 'My God, you should have seen him eat at the hotel!'

Jose heard what Rikki really said. About the food being pig's slop. The motor vehicle just an old rusty bucket. Worse. Rikki also swore constantly. Jose could understand Adolfo not wanting to translate the truth.

As the road became rougher and the vehicle lurched and

swayed, Senhor Jack fell silent. Jose held on to the dashboard and the handle on the side of the cabin, trying to steady his rocking body. The Blonde Lady kept brushing her yellow hair out of her face. 'Oh goodness,' she said many times.

Rikki had stopped his swearing and insulting remarks and now concentrated on guiding the vehicle between the ruts and large craters in the road. Jose peered into his paper bag. Only a couple of cubes of chewing gum left. He fished out one of the green-and-yellow wrapped pieces just as Rikki announced that Ermera was close by.

'This is the village of my father and mother!' Adolfo said. 'My father was an official here before the war.' He turned around to face Jose. 'This is where we all lived until your mother met your father.'

'What happened to Jose's father?' the Blonde Lady asked. 'I heard that he was killed in an accident . . .'

'The army jeep overturned. On a road in the mountains near here. There were two others in the jeep but only Domingo was killed.'

'But that's tragic!' the Blonde Lady said.

'Domi was an officer, you know. He was going to take my sister and Jose back to Portugal to meet his family.'

'Where did Mother and Tia Amelia live, Adolfo?'

'Oh, there was a big house on the other side of Ermera. Near the church. You can't see it from here.'

Suddenly, the overpowering aroma of rabusta coffee hit his nose. Jose remembered the smell so clearly. It was everywhere in Ermera. And there was Tia Amelia's roasting chicken and pork too, and Uncle Tschia pressing a gold coin into his hand the day Jose was confirmed at the big church on the hill, Our Lady of Fatima. The coin was safe and snug with his other precious possessions. With his father's picture, hidden at the back of the drawer in his room.

Ermera was on the other side of the ridge and they didn't see much of the town, just a few houses and people passing by. One or two of them raised their arms in greeting, but the Land Rover continued on over the crest of a small mountain range and into a number of deep valleys. The vehicle was travelling along a rough road now at considerable speed, and the place Jose had made for himself became extremely uncomfortable. He seemed to be sitting on nuts and bolts. Several times, the tool box moved and crushed against his leg. Jose had difficulty shifting it. Then one of the spare tyres came loose and Rikki had to stop the vehicle to lift it back into place and tie it tight with rope. They had a ten minute rest at Atsabe, a tiny village, the houses perched side-by-side on the deep slope of the hill.

'Another three hours,' Rikki said, pulling on his gloves.
'Another three hours,' Adolfo told Senhor Jack.
Again the road climbed, the lush undergrowth giving way to a sparsely vegetated plain. Adolfo was excited now, peering out the window, then leaning across the Blonde Lady to look out the other side. 'Soon, soon,' he said, 'soon we will see it.'
'What will we see, Tio?'
'My Tree of Life!'
'His Tree of Lies!' Rikki quipped from the front.
It was early evening and the light was fading. 'How will we find the tree in the dark?' Jose asked.

'Stop! Stop! Stop!' Adolfo suddenly yelled in English. He looked about wildly, his eyes large. 'It must be here.'

The vehicle lurched to a halt. Adolfo was the first out. To one side of the road was a deep gully while on the other side a flat area was bordered by a line of trees.

'They're eucalypts!' Senhor Jack said enthusiastically. 'Look Judy, just like in Australia.'

'Don't be silly, Jack. They can't be!' The Blonde Lady said. She had her arms wrapped about her shoulders. 'Besides, I'm cold, Jack. Freezing.'

'Look, look, they are.' Senhor Jack took a few steps and bent down to strip the leaves off a fallen branch. He rubbed the leaves between his palms. 'Here, Judy, just smell it.'

The Blonde Lady bowed her head to the leaves and inhaled. 'You're right.'

'I mean, it makes sense, the seeds blowing across the Timor Sea.'

Jose peered at the trees in the fading light. They were just trees. He had seen them before. There were many in the hills behind Baucau.

But Adolfo was already a good distance down the road, past the line of the trees. Jose ran after him. 'It must be here, I remember, it must be here. Just past the trees.' His head snapped from side to side. 'It must be, it must!'

'Is it a big tree, Tio?' said Jose in pursuit.

'It was a big tree, once, a long time ago. It was a stump with black bark . . .' He stopped, his whole body tense. He pointed. 'There, there it is!'

The lone stump with its dark bark stood out against the

light grey of the grassy open space. There was another long line of trees a little further on.

'Is this the Tree of Life, Tio?'

'The Tree, the Tree,' Adolfo said softly, and sighed. 'The Tree.' And then he started to run again. For a moment, Jose couldn't move as he watched his uncle running across the thigh-high grass towards the Tree. Then the others followed, all running.

The bark was black and crusty, fire-charred, the trunk as high as Senhor Jack. The top looked to Jose as though some giant hand had snapped it off and thrown it to one side. A large section of it lay near by, half rotten.

'Where is the entrance?' asked Jose.

'Quiet! You're too impatient. We will find it in a moment.'

Adolfo walked around the trunk, examining it carefully. Occasionally he would touch it gently, and several times he banged on it with a closed fist. The Blonde Lady stood silently and watched, while Senhor Jack was clutching his belly, trying to catch his breath. Rikki stood well back. He looked angry.

Then Adolfo gave out a small cry. He had found what he was looking for, a small opening at the base of the trunk. The hole had been covered up by vegetation. He pulled at the foliage and after a moment the opening enlarged.

'My God!' the Blonde Lady gasped. 'You hid in *there* for two whole days?'

Adolfo straightened up. Jose noticed his shoulders squared, as if he was standing at attention, like the soldiers at the barracks. But his stance only lasted a moment.

'Tio?' It was as if Adolfo was in a trance.

'It's all right,' he said.

His hat had fallen off and he jammed it back on with both hands. He simply nodded. He pointed back towards the line of eucalypts. 'Senhor Red and another man were carrying a wounded man up from the valley, and we didn't know the Japanese were hiding there, up on the hill. They shot at us and we ran. Senhor Red was safe with the others but I had a big bag and couldn't run fast enough. Senhor Red came back after the others were safe in the trees. We could see the Japanese coming and we crawled into the trunk.'

Jose's chest swelled as he listened to his uncle. He noticed Rikki still standing to one side, hands deep in the pockets of his shorts, peering down at the grass as if he was looking for something.

'After the shooting stopped, the Japanese came back to the Tree and made a fire and cooked food. We could smell the food and heard them talk. When morning came, Senhor Red and I were frightened and we stayed another night. After that, we walked to Bobonaro to join the other Australian soldiers.'

'You did not eat, Tio, in the Tree?'

'No Jose. We only had a canteen of water.'

Senhor Jack walked around the Tree. 'So this is the one the old man hid in. It was about the only thing he mentioned from the war. He was funny about it. Just held it close to his chest.'

Then Senhor Jack was beside Adolfo and had his arm around him. 'I'm grateful, Adolfo, really grateful that the old man had a friend like you.'

The gesture was too much for Rikki. It was as if he understood what was being said. 'All lies, lies, lies!' he yelled in Tetum. 'No man can live inside a tree for two days!'

Without answering, Adolfo dropped onto his knees, brushed the hat from his head and with a swift movement, disappeared through the opening. The Blonde Lady sucked her breath in sharply.

Senhor Jack bent down to peer into the hole but his big belly made the movement awkward. He shouted into the opening: 'You all right in there, Adolfo?'

There was no answer, only a scratching sound.

'You all right?'

No answer.

The scratching noise again.

'Tio? Tio?' Jose said. He was on his hands and knees, trying to peer into the opening.

Something emerged. Jose took it from Tio Adolfo's hand and tried to see what it was, but the light was failing. He handed it up to Senhor Jack.

'What the . . .' Senhor Jack said. He turned the object over and over. 'It's an army canteen, for Christ's sake. All rusted but the webbing is still in place.'

Adolfo's hand again emerged. This time it held what looked like a long knife. Jose passed it to Senhor Jack.

'Christ, a bayonet!'

Senhor Jack held the two objects in his hand and stared down at them as Adolfo emerged and straightened up. His face and clothes were covered with dirt. He wiped a hand across his mouth and nose. 'The truth of the Tree,' he said.

Jose looked across to Rikki. 'The Tree of Life exists.'

Rikki turned his head away as if he was searching for something on the other side of the clearing. 'The Tree of Life exists,' Rikki said softly, nodding his head. He started to walk back towards the vehicle.

For a few moments, they all stood in silence before the trunk and then Senhor Jack, handing the bayonet and canteen to Adolfo, tried to take a photo with his small camera but said the light was bad and the picture wouldn't come out. 'I left the flash back in the car,' he said.

'Go get it, Jack,' the Blonde Lady said. 'You've got to get a shot of the tree!'

'It'll be pitch-black by the time I get back!'

'Well, try with the camera at least.'

'All right, I'll give it a go.' He made some adjustments on the camera, his eyes almost touching it as he tried to see. Then he stepped back and snapped a couple of shots.

'All right,' he said at last, and pushed the camera into its case. He slung it over his shoulder. 'Let's go!'

'It's such an incredible place,' the Blonde Lady said, sniffing, as if she was trying not to cry. 'To think that people died here, killed each other . . .'

'Come on, Judy . . .' Senhor Jack said.

As they walked slowly back to the vehicle, the Blonde Lady had her handkerchief pressed to her mouth and Senhor Jack put his arm around her shoulder.

The road climbed again. Rikki drove with intense concentration, Jose noticed, and the sarcastic remarks, the insults, had all stopped. Then Rikki pointed with his gloved hand at a handful of sparkling lights in the distance. 'Maliana,' he said.

Jose was sleepy. He could hardly keep his eyes open; his chin kept dropping down to his chest and only the pain of his neck pulled him awake. His body ached from the cramped seat and his buttocks had become numb. It can't be far now, he kept thinking.

'Soon, soon,' Rikki said, his head and upper body a ghostly silhouette in the glow of the headlights.

'What did he say?' Senhor Jack asked.

'Balibo, very soon!' Adolfo replied. And after a while: 'Balibo!'

Jose moaned in the dark. His body hurt.

'God, what a trip!' the Blonde Lady said.

'Tio? Is it far now?'

'Only a little distance,' Adolfo said.

The vehicle pulled into a square and Jose could just make out a number of houses. Rikki stopped in front of a low, long building, its windows yellow with lights. A man in a white uniform stood on the steps, the Chef de Posto, and beside him a woman.

'We'll see you in the morning,' Senhor Jack said as he jumped out. As Rikki unloaded the bags, Adolfo turned and said: 'We will sleep in the guest house, on the far side of the square.'

Jose looked out the window. The Blonde Lady was on the steps of the house, shaking hands with the Chef de Posto and the Senhora. The vehicle dipped slightly as Rikki jumped back into the driver's seat. A screech of gears, a short drive and they were ushered into a big, thatched house; more like a large room, with beds in rows against the walls and a large table and chairs in the middle. On the far side of the room was a shelf on which stood a number of Balinese statues, just the head and shoulders of men and women. Several candles had been placed before the carvings and a slight movement of air made the lights dance.

Jose thought the faces were laughing.

9

Rendezvous at Batugade

For a few moments, Jose tried not to move as he watched a giant spider crawl along the ceiling. A red body and long legs. The ceiling was high with thick crossbeams. *Where am I?*

Then a familiar sound hit his ear.

On the cot beside him, flat on his back and dressed only in his khaki shorts, Adolfo snored loudly. Jose let his eyes roam around the room. There were two rows of bunks stretching along either side. Further up, Jose made out the sleeping form of Rikki. He was on his back, one hand stuck out still wearing the stained glove. At the end of the long dormitory he could see the shelf with the row of Balinese statues.

Balibo! Now it all came back.

Jose eased his legs over the side of the wooden bed and slipped into his sandals, then fastened the buckles. As he moved towards the door, he scooped his T-shirt from the adjoining bed and pulled it over his head only when he stood outside the door.

The day was already bright. A cock crowed from somewhere between two palm-thatched houses, and further down the road a number of women scuttled about, their torsos wrapped in brightly coloured cloths. Several people wished him a good morning. He turned and looked along the row of houses. There it was! A fort, with battlements and cannons sticking out, pointing over the grey-green trees, dominating the village. A grand house with white walls and big doors had been built at the foot of the fort. The villa of the Chef de Posto. The Land Rover was parked outside.

The fort. He had to see the fort. Were there soldiers at the fort? Manning the guns to fight off attackers? He moved past the Chef de Posto's villa and the Land Rover and walked up the narrow ramp until he stood right in the half-circle confines of the fortifications. The big cannons, rusty and encrusted, were propped against the stone wall. One of the guns, however, was positioned out over the battlements. He climbed up and, sitting astride, he had a clear view of the broad road which passed through the middle of a cluster of houses. They weren't built in a neat and tidy row as they were in Baucau, but were scattered, one facing this way, the other that.

The sun was bright and golden red and, by shielding his eyes, he could see the blue-white sparkle of the sea in the distance. Sister Philomena had spoken about the brave Portuguese sailors who had steered their boats through these uncharted seas. Large boats, with billowing sails, and loaded with gold and spices, sailing on the seas with the wind blowing strong. 'I will protect you, from up here, up here in the mountains, on this hill fortress with my men and guns . . .'

'It must be one of the loveliest spots on earth,' the Blonde Lady said beside him. Jose half turned and nearly tumbled from the cannon in surprise. 'Lovely, lovely,' she said and shook her head. 'Your uncle and Rikki are still asleep?'

He nodded. 'Yes, Senhora. He likes his sleep when he doesn't have to clean the pool.' He wondered how the Blonde Lady had got up here without him noticing.

She looked out over the hills towards the sea, then said: 'The Administrator is taking Jack pigeon shooting this morning.' She smiled at him. 'I bet you would like to go with them, eh?'

'Oh yes, Senhora, yes.' He had never been on a pigeon shoot.

'They say the pigeons make fine eating. But I guess that's not what you're interested in. Am I right?'

'Yes, Senhora. Will Tio Adolfo come too?'

'Of course. It'll be a task to separate you two!'

'Adolfo will show me how to use a gun.'

'Now I don't know about that,' she said and smiled.

'Adolfo knows how to handle a gun.'

'I'm sure he does.' She moved to the edge of the wall and placed a hand on the rusted cannon. 'I'm going to spend time with Senhora Famia, the Chef de Posto's wife. It must be lonely for her, up here in the hills.' She sighed. 'Such a beautiful place, this area. So lovely. It's hard to believe that the Portuguese have been here over four hundred years. Can you imagine, just seventy years after Christopher

Columbus discovered America? Amazing how far people travelled in those days . . .'

Sister Philomena had spoken about Christopher Columbus and there was a drawing of him in one of Jose's schoolbooks. But he sailed under the Spanish flag, not the Portuguese. He knew about Henry the Navigator too, one of Portugal's great princes. But he didn't want to think about Columbus or Henry the Navigator now. He wanted to talk about the pigeon hunt.

'Will Senhor Jack fire a gun?'

'Of course. You mean on the pigeon shoot?' Then she added, 'You love your uncle, don't you?'

'Yes, Senhora. He teaches me a lot of things. And we go to the cockfights together.'

'I think you'll miss him . . . when you go to Portugal.'

A sudden heaviness pushed down on his shoulders. He hadn't thought about it for a long time. He was going to leave Timor for Portugal.

'Yes, Senhora.'

'You'll do well there. You're a bright young man!'

Jose was silent.

'Jack and I've talked. We're going to help as much as we can.' She turned her head as if she had said something she hadn't wanted to.

Just then, Adolfo's shouts came from the bottom of the ramp. 'Jose! Jose, where are you?'

He pushed himself off the cannon. 'I must go, Senhora.'

A short time later, after a breakfast of omelette and bread, Jose crammed into the back of an open military vehicle with Tio Adolfo; Rikki was to stay behind – he had work to do on the Land Rover. Senhor Jack sat in front with the Chef de Posto driving. Behind them was another vehicle with three Timorese soldiers and a Portuguese officer. One of the soldiers carried a machine-gun.

The road out of Balibo, as soon as they had cleared the trees around the village, began to drop rapidly as it twisted and turned towards the sea. There was little vegetation other than an occasional small tree and a few low bushes. Brown-coloured ridges stretched above them and down towards the coastline. The road was no more than a narrow track in places.

After a while, Jose suddenly noticed that the engine had stopped its soft burr. 'We have no engine!' he yelled at Adolfo over the roar of the wind.

'The Senhor has switched it off to conserve petrol!'

'Why?'

'Petrol has to be brought up from Dili by truck. It is very valuable. Miguel sometimes makes the run for Old Wong. It is very good business.'

As the road stretched out on the flat coastal plain, the sparsely covered countryside and patches of grassland gave way to dense undergrowth and palm trees trying to out-do each other to reach light. They passed a small village, then what looked like a fortified village built in a clearing, within sound of the beating of the surf. There was a high fence of wire with towers dominating from the corners. Jose could see men in the towers looking down at them. The Portuguese flag flew above the main gate.

'Batugade!' The Chef de Posto said.

'Is it to guard the border?' Jose asked.

'Yes,' Adolfo said. 'The border is only a short distance away.'

'Will we go over the border into Indonesia?'

But no one answered.

They turned right, away from where Adolfo had indicated the border, and drove along a narrow roadway almost parallel with the coast. Here there were a few palm-thatched houses built almost right on the beach, shaded by coconut palms. Boats were drawn up on the sand. Jose thought the sand on the beach was the whitest he had ever seen. Even whiter than the sand on Dili harbour.

Senhor Jack looked at his watch. 'It's a bit early. Chang said he wouldn't be at the border before one.'

'Then we have plenty of time for the pigeons,' the Chef de Posto laughed nervously. With his black beard trimmed to a fine point, and a moustache that curled downwards under his nose, Jose thought he looked like one of the kings of Portugal he had seen in his schoolbooks.

'Do we have to drive far?' Senhor Jack asked.

'No, not very far. The swamp around Be Malai full of pigeons.' The Chef de Posto's English was halting and occasionally Adolfo helped out with a translation.

Soon after this the vehicle skidded to a halt. The Chef de Posto pointed towards a thick concentration of trees, and there was a lot of movement in the branches. He reached under his seat and drew out a shotgun. Senhor Jack too had a gun in his hand.

'Come,' the Portuguese said and jumped out of the vehicle, his face red with excitement. Senhor Jack heaved his big body out of the car and Jose thought that the sound of their running on the dry packed earth was like the beat of a big drum. 'Jose, you and Adolfo better stay with the vehicle,' Senhor Jack shouted over his shoulder.

Jose climbed down and squatted with his uncle on a patch of dry grass. The army vehicle with the soldiers had pulled up just behind them. Jose turned around and saw the officer running after Senhor Jack and the Chef de Posto, a shotgun held ready. The soldiers, however, crouched down beside their vehicle and the man with the machine-gun pointed the muzzle skywards. One of the soldiers waved towards Jose and smiled.

Several shots echoed through the trees. Jose heard Senhor Jack shout. Another couple of shots. Then silence.

'It sounds as if the hunt has been successful,' Adolfo said slowly, rolling himself a cigarette from a tear of newspaper. 'There are many pigeons around here.'

'Why don't *you* hunt, Tio? You can shoot very well, can't you?'

'I'm too old for it. My bones would creak if I ran about in the marsh.'

Moments later Senhor Jack emerged, grinning, holding two bloodied pigeons by the wings. The Chef de Posto was also a good shot. He threw his three pigeons on top of Senhor Jack's. Soon after, the officer from the army vehicle heaped another couple of birds onto the pile. The Portuguese officer had shot the most – five birds. As he threw them down to join the others, he pulled a camera from a bag he had stored in the military vehicle and insisted that Adolfo take a picture of the three of them with the pigeons. Then he waved for Jose and Adolfo to pose with the group while another soldier took the picture.

'The cook at the Posto will be busy with these beauties!' the officer said. He only spoke Portuguese and Senhor Jack kept shaking his head because he didn't understand.

Jose had expected soldiers to guard the border with Indonesia, but the bridge of wood and stone across the shallow waterway was deserted. The Portuguese flag flew on one side, the Indonesian on the other. Senhor Jack got out of the vehicle and looked about.

The Chef de Posto said in Portuguese: 'Strange that there are no guards! You can usually see them from this side.'

Senhor Jack shielded his eyes from the sun and looked towards the border bridge. 'I hope Chang didn't muck up! He's usually very reliable.'

'Who's Chang?' Jose asked.

'The oil engineer with Senhor Jack's company,' Adolfo explained in a whisper.

'But why is he coming from the Indonesian side of the border?'

'The oil company has engineers all over the island. They say there is much oil on the southern side of Timor. Especially on the Portuguese side.'

The Portuguese officer and two Timorese soldiers from the truck behind them stood by the side of the road. The third soldier remained in the back of the open vehicle, machine-gun pointed upwards as before.

Jose stood beside Adolfo. It seemed to Jose that everyone was turning their heads this way and that, nobody really sure what they were looking for.

Suddenly, Jose noticed the sound of a small engine from across the bridge, a light purr at first, then louder and louder. A lone motorcycle rider. As he came nearer, Jose realised it was a Chinese man, in a dark green shirt and long trousers. That was most unusual: few people in Timor wore long trousers. Except the tourists.

The rider made it across the bridge, then pulled up the bike almost at Senhor Jack's feet. There was a lot of dust and the Chef de Posto and the soldiers moved back a pace, coughing.

'Chang! How are you, matey?' Senhor Jack held out one hand while the other pounded the man's back. He seemed genuinely pleased to see him.

The Chinese man was trying to catch his breath. 'Good, good, Jack!' he said in English. 'I've got the survey plans, the whole lot.' Without getting off the motorcycle, he twisted his body to reach behind him. A large briefcase was tied on the rack above the rear wheel. With Senhor Jack helping to untie the rope, it was soon freed. It seemed very heavy as Senhor Jack took it off, then pulled open the flap, quickly fingering the papers. He lifted his head and nodded. 'Great, Chang, just great. Looks like it's all there.'

The man pointed towards the ridges above them. 'There are many armed men on both sides of the border, Jack,' he said. 'The Indonesians have army units just down the road. It's going to start real soon. Get the hell out of it back to Dili! The Indonesians said there's been shooting on the road past Batugade. They've got units already working this side of the border.'

'That was us shooting,' Senhor Jack said and his head rocked back in a burst of laughter. The Portuguese too started to laugh. Jose and Adolfo joined in. 'That was us hunting pigeons, Chang.' He turned and pointed to the pile of birds in the vehicle. 'Have a look at that!'

But Jose saw Chang shake his head. He obviously didn't see the humour in the situation. In fact he seemed angry: 'Shooting around here is bloody stupid! They'll think the fighting's started.'

'Who?'

'Apodeti fighters! Fretilin! Who knows. It's all so damned confusing.'

The hot-heads, Jose thought.

Chang kick-started the motorbike and on top of the noise he shouted: 'Best to drive back to Balibo!'

'Come on, Chang, nothing will happen . . .'

'Believe me, it's best to go, Jack. Get the hell out of it,' he said again, 'as soon as you can.' He put the machine into gear. 'Give my regards to the boys in Melbourne. We'll catch up soon. Have a beer and a talk!'

'Take care, Chang!'

They watched as Chang turned the motorcycle and headed back over the bridge. Finally all Jose could see was a distant cloud of dust.

'We better go,' the Chef de Posto said loudly in English.

They all scrambled back into the vehicles.

Jose looked out over the sea. He thought he could hear something. An engine, like the motorcycle. But it sounded different. The others too noticed it. The Chef de Posto, hand shielding his eyes, was searching the sky.

A helicopter clattered towards them over the deep blue-green of the flat ocean.

From the Indonesian side.

10

Flight to Balibo

Jose saw the helicopter clearly, skimming over the water, a mechanical bird without markings. Still some distance out to sea, it gradually tipped to its side and began to gain height until it was over them. Jose could make out two men in the cockpit, faces strangely illuminated, and there were two other men crouched in the open doorway. One of these was sitting on the sill filming them with a hand-held camera. The other man, half hidden, seemed to be carrying a gun.

Senhor Jack shielded his eyes from the sun as he peered up at the helicopter. 'I can't see any markings!' he yelled over the whine of the engine. 'They're Indonesians.'

The Chef de Posto didn't answer. His face had set itself into a mask and he concentrated on manoeuvring the bouncing, rattling vehicle over the many potholes and ridges on the narrow road. The other vehicle stayed close behind.

Senhor Jack shouted again over the noise of the engine, 'They're not going to shoot us!'

The Portuguese didn't take any notice.

This is what the troubles are all about, Jose thought. He was scared. 'Tio Adolfo?'

'Hold on, tight,' Adolfo said tensely. 'Hold on!'

Jose did hold on. He grabbed at the side of the vehicle and as it bounced over a particularly bad rut, he felt his body lift out of the seat, then come crashing down. Something hard connected with his hip. He winced in pain.

The Batugade outpost was up ahead. Jose saw clearly the closed gate and the wire fence and the watchtowers on the corners, and the Portuguese flag flying over the main gate. There was no sign of activity.

As the road left the narrow flat of the coast, it wound its way between sharp ridges, giant furrows cut into the earth which extended up the slope and looked as if they had been covered by brown rattan matting. Occasionally, a clump of waist-high bushes had sprung up in the depressed shallows where two ridges met.

The Chef de Posto crunched into another gear and the vehicle's engine whined in a higher pitch as it pulled upwards on the increasingly steeper slope.

Adolfo's hand was hot on Jose's arm. They watched the helicopter in the distance, hovering above the area where the border bridge was situated. Suddenly, as if obeying a command, it shot upwards and towards them. Jose again saw the brown faces peering down and for an instant, he wanted to raise his hand in a wave but decided against it. The man with the gun looked grim-faced.

The mechanical bird now made a wide sweep up towards Balibo and disappeared over the crest of the hill, only to appear again a little further down the coast on the Portuguese side. It then stopped in mid-air, as if it had found a target on the ground, and a moment later the sound of machine-gun fire echoed across the slopes.

'My God, they're shooting!' Senhor Jack yelled.

The radio under the dashboard crackled. Jose couldn't follow what it was about but the high-pitched shouts of someone were intermingled with the sound of the gun. 'They're shooting!' Senhor Jack repeated as he slumped back into his seat. And then he added, 'I hope it wasn't at Chang.'

The whole village seemed to be out on the road as they drove into Balibo. The vehicle with the soldiers was still close behind. The Blonde Lady and Senhora Famia were standing on the steps of the Casa de Posto and as they stopped and Senhor Jack jumped down, his wife rushed towards him.

'Oh Jack, you all right?' she cried. Jose thought she seemed very upset. 'We heard shooting and then the radio...'

'It's all right, we're all right.'

'I've been so worried.'

'We're leaving. Right now. Get your things together. Where's Rikki?'

'With the Land Rover.'

'Good! Half an hour and we're out of this place.'

'Why, Jack, what happened?'

'I think they were just trying to scare us. Give us a warning.' He hesitated a moment. 'It looked as though they might have been after Chang. But it was too far away to really be sure.'

'No! You mean the geologist? The man I met with you in Melbourne?'

'Yes.'

'Oh Jack, you don't think he's dead?'

'I'm not saying he's dead. But they *were* shooting. On the Indonesian side. They followed him after he gave me the satchel.'

She suddenly became angry, moved away from Senhor Jack and put her hands on her hips. 'The bloody oil company.'

'Well, there's no real reason to think they've got him. He's probably safe and okay.' He reached out and tried to take hold of her, but she moved a step back.

'You're all playing with each other's lives. No job is worth that much.'

Jose felt Adolfo's arm on his shoulder. 'We must go, Jose. This is no place for us.'

Jose understood what he was saying. He watched the Blonde Lady's face.

'We must get our things. Hurry!'

'Will there be fighting here? Will they shoot at us?' asked Jose.

'No, but we must go. Quickly!'

As they hurried towards the dormitory at the side of the Casa de Posto, Jose saw Rikki in the doorway. The usual arrogant sneer which played at the corner of his mouth was gone. He looked frightened.

* * *

There were four soldiers sitting at the table in the dormitory, playing cards. A large black transistor radio was propped up on a bed. It was one of the biggest Jose had ever seen.

'What happened at Batugade?' one of them wanted to know.

Jose quickly told them about the helicopter and the shooting.

'Indonesians!' one said.

'Apodeti and UDT don't have helicopters,' another said.

A black Angolan asked Jose in halting Tetum: 'You're Captain Domingo's boy?'

'Yes . . .' Jose began.

'We were in Africa together.' He smiled as he extended a hand. 'I'm pleased to meet with Captain Domingo's son.'

Jose placed his hand in the soldier's. The man's fist felt abnormally large and it swallowed Jose's hand. The soldier laughed.

The music on the radio all of a sudden changed. One of the soldiers laid down his cards, then reached over to the bed to adjust the dial. The music stopped. Jose recognised the language as Bahasa Indonesian, but he didn't really understand what the man was saying. He asked Adolfo.

'It's Radio Australia. The news!' his uncle said crisply.

The man on the radio spoke for a long time and finally he stopped, and the music came on again.

'What did the news say, Tio?'

'It didn't say anything important.'

'Did the news come from Australia?'

'Yes, from Australia,' the Angolan soldier laughed. His teeth were very white. 'A long way, eh?'

'Darwin?'

'No, no, much further!'

'Sydney?'

'No, much further than even Sydney. Melbourne.'

'Where's Melbourne?'

'Long way. Right at the bottom of Australia. Very far.'

The soldier at the radio leaned closer, his ear almost touching the speaker. He twisted the tiny knob and a babble of voices, men and women, flooded the dormitory. Then one voice, clear and without crackling, came over the radio. Jose recognised the language as English, though he didn't understand exactly what was being said. The man seemed to be describing a sporting event.

'Football!' one of the soldiers said. 'From Melbourne!'

'A lot of the Australians came from Melbourne. During the war,' Adolfo added, and scratched at his face. 'They always talked about it.'

'Soccer? Like they play in Portugal?'

Adolfo shook his head. 'No, not soccer. They play their football with an oval ball.' He motioned with his hand. 'Like an egg! A tourist told me about it.'

As Jose and Adolfo made towards the Land Rover parked in front of the Chef de Posto's villa, the engine of the vehicle running, he saw Rikki in the driver's seat with his gloved hands on the wheel. The egg-shaped football still preoccupied Jose's thoughts.

It seemed ridiculous, playing with a football the shape of an egg.

11

Adolfo Buys a Bird

Without warning, the vehicle tipped to one side and came to a violent stop as if it had hit a wall. Jose flew out of his seat and his shoulder connected painfully with the rear door. Cartons and boxes overturned – there was a lot of noise. The Blonde Lady gave a startled cry. Then all was still. Jose blinked as the late afternoon sun slanted into the cabin, highlighting tiny speckles of dust. As Senhor Jack coughed and tried to open the door, the Land Rover lurched forward as if something had pushed it hard from behind, then came to rest with the front passenger side angled precariously downwards.

'Oh!' the Blonde Lady said, her voice now curiously calm.

'You all right?' Senhor Jack asked.

'What happened?'

'Dunno!' Senhor Jack turned in the seat. 'Is everyone all right?' He tried to open his door but it was jammed. Rikki still held on to the steering wheel with one hand; the other hand made frantic motions.

Jose, in the back, peered out the rear window. All he could see were trees. He worked the handle but the door didn't budge. Adolfo was the calmest. 'A big hole,' he said without raising his voice. Pushing against his door, he managed to open it and helped the Blonde Lady out, then made his way around the back to get Jose.

They all formed a half circle around the nose of the Land Rover and stared down at the large pothole into which its wheel had sunk. The hole was deep enough to tip the vehicle's wheel on the opposite side high off the ground.

Rikki broke the silence. He made digging motions with his gloved hands and said in Tetum: 'Dig, we must dig it out! Stones, wood, anything to lift the wheel.' Adolfo translated and Senhor Jack nodded. There was a small spade in the vehicle and Rikki now set to, shovelling stones and sand into the hole. Senhor Jack then got some equipment from the back of the vehicle. 'Here,' he said to Jose, 'help me carry this to the front!'

Jose grabbed the lever of a tyre jack and followed him up to the front of the Land Rover. Senhor Jack handed him a long piece of wood. 'This might help!'

The road they were on ran parallel to a dry riverbed and there was an abundance of stones. As the hole gradually filled, Rikki fitted a long grey stone under the vehicle as a base for the tyre jack. As he worked the lever, the wheel lifted and another stone was pushed under it. It was slow, heavy work and Senhor Jack's face and upper body were wet, as if someone had thrown a bucket of water over him.

The Blonde Lady warned him several times. 'Jack, take it easy, will you. I don't want you to collapse with a heart attack!'

'Won't be long.'

The wheel was now almost level with the road surface. Rikki put one more stone under it and worked the jack again.

Suddenly Jose stepped back, startled. Two men stood beside him, chests bare, their black skins glistening with sweat in the hot, humid air. The taller of the two carried a clump of edible roots over one shoulder, a large knife balanced on the other. The shorter man wore an elaborate headgear of feathers and carried a cock. He had the blackest face Jose had ever seen. Only Sister Philomena's was blacker.

Senhor Jack was also startled by their appearance. 'Where did these two come from?'

The man with the knife spoke excitedly in a dialect Jose didn't recognise.

Adolfo translated. 'They're puzzled, Senhor!' He wiped sweat from his forehead with an arm. 'They have never been in a motor vehicle. They can't see the ponies pulling it.'

Senhor Jack's big body shook with laughter, his sack-like stomach moved from side to side as if filled with water. 'Did you hear that, Judy? No ponies!'

'Oh Jack!' The Blonde Lady sat down on a large log at the side of the road. She lashed at the flies with her scarf. 'Why don't we just get out of this place. It gives me the creeps.'

The tall man pointed the knife towards a hill behind them, his eyes wide as he spoke.

'What's he saying, Adolfo?'

'He says there are armed men in the hills. He says the men are ready for war. They have many weapons.'

'Where are they now?'

'About five kilometres back. We must go quickly!'

'You don't have to tell me that.'

The man with the headdress suddenly thrust the cock bird towards Adolfo.

'He wants to give you a cock, Tio!' Jose said.

'He doesn't want to give it to me, he wants to *sell* it.'

'Why?'

'Because he's hungry. The fighting is interfering with the crops.'

Adolfo pushed at the bird with a palm as he spoke, but in mid sentence he stopped and looked curiously at the bird. He reached out and with a finger stroked its head, almost with affection, making small sounds with his lips. It was a young cock and looked thin and undernourished, but its feathers were dirt-brown and flecked with red and gold; the tail, though short, the colours of the rainbow. As the bird twitched its head, Adolfo let out a soft 'Aeee-eh!'

The man knew then that he had Adolfo's interest. Quickly he put the cock down on the sandy road. For a moment, the cock's eyes twitched around and up, then it took a couple of uncertain jerky steps. As it became used to the ground, the steps became surer.

'Ai-eh!' Adolfo hissed between his teeth. 'Aiee,' he said again and held his head.

'What is it, Tio?'

'The bird, the bird . . .'

'What about the bird?'

'It is a fine bird!'

Senhor Jack had bent down to see how Rikki was doing at the wheel. When he heard Adolfo hiss, he lifted his head. 'What's the matter with you? Come on, let's get at that wheel. It's nearly out.'

Adolfo didn't answer. Instead, he squatted down before the bird and cupped its wings. Immediately, the bird's neck feathers came up. Almost in a whisper, Adolfo said, 'Look, Jose, look! Look how strong his legs are!'

'Adolfo, come on mate, give us a hand here,' urged Senhor Jack.

Jose watched his uncle. Tio Adolfo seemed too fascinated by the bird to answer. 'This could be a wondrous fighting cock,' he said, and turned to Jose. His voice trembled with awe. Then a grin broke out on his face. He grinned and grinned and his face began to twitch with the effort. 'It is a great bird!'

Senhor Jack straightened up, wiping his face with his shirtsleeve. 'Adolfo! What's going on? We've got to get going, mate.'

Rikki too stood and began packing the equipment back into the Land Rover. Senhor Jack watched in silence, not sure what he should do.

'It is a great bird, Senhor,' Adolfo repeated.

Senhor Jack seemed angry. He gulped air. 'Don't worry about the bloody bird.'

It was as if Tio Adolfo hadn't heard. Jose and he just

stared at the bird, transfixed. Then Adolfo asked the Timorese something.

'He wants fifty escudos!' Adolfo said.

To one side, Rikki exploded in laughter.

Senhor Jack, gruffly: 'That's nothing!'

Rikki had difficulty controlling his mirth. 'A skinny, bony bird, good for soup!'

Tio Adolfo was speaking softly with the man. Finally, he said: 'Thirty escudos.'

Senhor Jack thrust a handful of notes at Adolfo. 'Here, matey, give him the bloody money and let's get the hell out of here. This place makes me nervous!'

'It is still expensive.'

'Who cares. Let's just go!'

Rikki was already behind the wheel and the engine had started. The Blonde Lady too had got in quickly.

'Come on, Adolfo, let's go!'

Senhor Jack's shout finally ripped Adolfo out of his trance. He pushed the notes into the Timorese man's outstretched hand and almost in one motion bent down and took the bird into his arms.

Rikki leaned out of the window and shouted, 'The cock is not a bargain! It's a *mountain* cock. A coward! Heeeii-ih!' He slapped the side of the vehicle and it sounded like shots. 'Mountain cocks have no courage... Even the soup they make is sour!'

The Timorese began walking up the road, the colourful feather headdress swaying. Jose thought it looked as if the man actually had a bird sitting on his head.

Adolfo had climbed in, carefully nursing the bird in his

arms. The gears crunched and the vehicle slowly moved forward. Between shifting gears, Rikki burst into little giggles. When at last the Land Rover moved at an even pace on the road parallel to the river, the giggles turned into hysterical laughter. His legs wobbled and his arms, thin sticks with their gloved hands, flapped about imitating the wings of a bird.

'Why is he laughing, Tio?' asked Jose. He agreed with Adolfo – it looked like a fine bird.

'He thinks the bird is a great joke.' Adolfo was stroking the bird's head.

Rikki's antics irritated Senhor Jack. He turned, his face red. 'What's the matter with him?'

'He's laughing,' Tio Adolfo said, stern-faced.

'I can see that! But why?'

'He's laughing at me, Senhor Jack. Because of the cock!'

'The cock?'

'It is a mountain bird. Rikki says it's a coward.'

'Oh for Christ's sake . . .'

Rikki kept up his ridicule. As he drove, he flicked his gloved hand towards Adolfo sitting with the cock in the back of the vehicle, and once in a while let out an hysterical shriek.

Finally, Senhor Jack lost his temper. 'Tell him to *cut* it, will you? I can't stand this bloody nonsense anymore!'

'He's only having fun,' the Blonde Lady said.

'It's driving me insane.'

'Jack!'

Rikki continued. 'Adolfo, mad Adolfo and his mountain cock!'

'You are evil, Rikki!'

'And *you* are mad.'

Senhor Jack slammed his fist into the side of the vehicle and shouted: 'For Christ's sake, shut your mouths, both of you!' Jose jumped.

During the hours it took to reach Dili, Adolfo sat with the bird cradled in his arms like a babe asleep. Soon it was dark. Several times, as the headlights reflected against the dense undergrowth and the cabin was illuminated just for a moment with a strange glow, Jose watched as the bird rubbed its beak along Adolfo's brown arm. He wanted to ask Tio Adolfo a hundred questions, but he kept his silence when he saw tears in his uncle's eyes.

12

Tongues Wagging

As Jose and Adolfo walked up the gravelled road on the second day after they got back to Baucau, his uncle carried the bird firmly pressed into his side. As they passed the Posada on the way to the pool, Toni the gardener shouted as he saw them coming. He stopped sweeping the steps and a broad grin split his face. 'Bon Dia. How's the little fighter?'

Adolfo didn't break his stride but only shifted the pole from one shoulder to the other and moved the bird against his belly. 'He does well, Toni, and it's good of you to ask!'

'He can help you clean the pool!' He cackled loudly.

Adolfo kept his silence.

'There are good cocks to be bought in the Bobonaro high country. But only good for soup!'

'Your advice is not wanted.'

'No, it's not wanted!' Jose said. He had helped Adolfo take care of the cock since their return. He had a say in this conversation.

'The cocks from the high country have no heart,' Toni continued. 'The air is much too cool for them. They lack spirit.'

'We don't need your words,' Adolfo returned.

'Heiiii!' And Toni took up his broom again and continued sweeping.

When Jose arrived at school, his mind was full of the bird. He wanted to tell Carmillo and the others about the Bobonaro bird, but some invisible finger stilled his lips. After school, Carmillo left the classroom quickly and then through the window Jose saw him waiting at the gate, the other boys around him. So Jose shuffled about the classroom, cleaning the blackboard, delaying going out into the yard as long as possible. Sister Philomena finally shouted at him: 'Out!' He ran into the yard but couldn't see Carmillo. All of them had gone. He started to run along the gravelled road towards the Posada.

Adolfo was on the far side, working the edge of the pool with his pole, and beyond him the bird was pecking at worms in the shade of a palm.

As Jose ran down the stairway, a loud cry snapped up his head. Carmillo, face puffed red in anger, stood on top of the parapet, hands on his bulky hips, shouting obscenities. He was back in full form.

'Aee-ie! The cock from the hills will run like a coward!' he yelled.

Adolfo pulled the pole from the water and waved at Jose to hurry down. 'They are only words,' he said impatiently when Jose got there, short of breath. 'Pay no attention to them.'

Jose was surprised at his uncle's calmness.

'We have much work to do with the bird,' Adolfo said, more to himself than Jose.

Up above, Carmillo, getting no reaction, finally gave up his shouting and moved away.

Adolfo had secured the bird to a stake with a piece of coloured string. As Jose squatted down beside it, he reached out and the bird pecked his finger. He pulled back quickly.

'He has a fighter's spirit, Jose.'

'My finger is bleeding!'

Adolfo laughed.

'Will you fight it, Tio?'

'You keep asking me the same questions, Jose!'

'Well?'

'It is only a young bird. Weak, with no muscles. It must grow a little before we decide.'

'When will you know?'

'Soon!' Adolfo said brusquely.

'But when, Tio, *when*?'

Adolfo picked up his pole and moved towards the pool. 'It is natural for a cock to fight. I will decide soon.'

The large figure of Miguel appeared up on the steps. Jose knew that his stepfather must have finished the food haul to Lautem, but he seldom came down to the pool. As he moved towards them, he scratched at his stomach. 'There is a lot of talk at Old Wong's store,' he said. 'Is this the cock they are all talking about?'

Jose didn't answer. Three pairs of eyes watched the cock peck at the ground. Then, as Miguel moved an arm towards it, the bird's colour-streaked neck feathers flared. 'Ei-eh!' Miguel said in surprise.

'He is a fighting cock!' Adolfo said, and turned away to fiddle with the pole.

Jose thought his stepfather was impressed. But typically of him, he wasn't going to give in to Adolfo. 'I see only a skinny cock from up-country,' he said solemnly. 'Birds from up-country have no courage. You should know that, Adolfo! A fighter needs courage and endurance.' He rubbed his temple. 'He will be a coward in a fight.'

Adolfo shook his head vigorously. 'He is a fighter, you will see!'

'Yes, look at the way he moves,' Jose said. He desperately wanted his stepfather to believe in the bird.

'I see no fighting spirit, only a skinny bird. Skinny with no muscles,' Miguel said.

'But he has spirit!' Jose returned.

'I don't see spirit in the bird! I see fear.' Then he stood up and again rubbed his stomach. 'It was foolish of you to buy the bird, Adolfo. The whole of Baucau will soon know about your bird, and people are laughing.' He shuffled across the lawn towards the stairway, moving his head from side to side as if he couldn't quite believe what Adolfo had done.

By the evening, most people in Baucau did know about the cock. Toni the gardener from the Posada told his wife and she in turn told the women who washed their family clothes in the concrete troughs behind the marketplace. The women there told their men. When she arrived home, Theresa could barely contain her anger. As they sat around the kitchen table, she smashed down a large bowl and shouted: 'You mad dog, Brother! Why do you have to dishonour this house?'

'It is a fighting bird,' Jose said. 'It will grow strong and become a good fighter!'

'All this talk about fighting cocks! Bah!'

Adolfo didn't raise his head once, all through the meal. When he finished he rose silently and moved out of the room. Jose wanted to follow his uncle, to go with him to the rear of the house and see the bird, but his mother's cold stare rooted him to his chair.

'Why does he *do* it?' Theresa said as if in pain and hit her forehead with the flat of her hand.

Jose looked at Miguel and thought: *he's* seen the bird at the pool and how its neck feathers flared! Why doesn't he *say* something?

'Ay-iiie!' Miguel moaned and kept sucking on his bottle of beer, trying not to look up. Miguel never said much at the table.

13

Training

'What about Senhor Jack? Will he come again with the Blonde Lady?' Jose asked when Adolfo told him by the pool days later that they had flown out of Baucau.

'Senhor Jack is in the south with his oil men. He will be back soon.' Adolfo laid down his pole and wiped his face with a rag. He looked at Jose with a curious expression. 'The Blonde Lady, well . . .!'

Jose's heart missed a beat. He sensed something. 'What Tio, tell me?'

'The Blonde Lady has flown home to Australia on the TAA aircraft from Dili. She will come again when it is time for you to leave for Portugal.'

Jose began to tremble. He couldn't see the sun. And it was chilly. 'Leaving for Portugal!' He had forgotten about it during the excitement of the last week.

'You mustn't think about it now, Jose. It will happen soon enough. We have much work to do with the bird.'

'But Portugal . . .'

Gently, Adolfo took his arm. 'Think about it when the time comes. Now help me with the bird!' He pulled something from behind the tree, a parcel of bright cloth. 'See?' Carefully, he folded back the strips. 'This will make the bird strong.'

Jose gasped. It was a crude glove made from a thick piece of canvas and as Adolfo fitted the folds over his right hand the bird blinked nervously, instantly alert, still tied by the string to the stake. Adolfo moved the glove in a circular motion before the bird's eyes. 'It must move to the left, always to the *left*, and then attack!' As if it heard the command, the bird swayed to the side.

'Why to the left?'

Adolfo smiled. 'It is a trick we are teaching it. To fool his opponent!'

'Can I try, Tio?'

'No, not now. In a couple of days when the bird has become used to the glove.'

Jose sat in the shade and watched the bird. If he was helping to train the bird, he thought, wouldn't the bird also be partly his?

At school in the early afternoon when the room was stifling hot, Jose watched the back of Carmillo's fat head, the straight black hair glistening as though wet. Fat-head! Fat hair! Fat face! Jose giggled. Why hadn't he thought of it before? Fat dripping over his face, over Carmillo's head, yellow as butter, palm oil, smearing it all over his fat . . . He hated Carmillo, hated him because he was a bully and his father was arrogant and owned all the good fighting cocks in Baucau. But he didn't want to think about Carmillo. He wanted to think about the bird, the training, the glove and how Adolfo trained it to move to the left... The bird had no name! No name!

A loud crack startled him awake. The side of his head exploded in pain. Sister Philomena's black face loomed over him. 'Night time is for dreaming, the day is for school!' And again, the pink underside of her giant hand swished down. Through the pain he heard the class erupt in laughter.

When he arrived at the pool after school, the side of his face was still smarting. Adolfo was working the bird, teasing it with the glove, making it move to the left, to the left, always to the left. There was a crowd up on the parapet – Baucau people and a couple of Timorese soldiers. A lone tourist too, a young man with a yellow beard, stood fascinated with what his uncle was doing. Jose was surprised to see the tourist. Miguel had said only a couple of nights ago that tourists stayed away from Timor now. There were sporadic outbreaks of fighting in the hills near the border.

'They are watching us, Tio!' he said when he stood beside Adolfo.

'If they have nothing better to do!'

'Can I try with the glove?'

'No, not yet. It must learn the right moves. There is no time for playing!'

'Tio?' Jose hesitated.

'Well, speak, if you must!'

'Tio, the bird. The bird is your bird? *Your* fighting cock?'

'It hasn't proven itself to be worthy of being called a fighting cock.'

But Jose remembered he'd said as much to Miguel. 'It is *your* bird then?'

Adolfo looked at him curiously, then pulled the canvas hat down further over his eyes. 'If you help in the training and share the work, naturally it belongs to both of us.'

'Our fighting cock!' Jose said to himself, his heart racing.

'Come, there is much work to do!'

Attack, counter-move, attack again, veering to the left, always to the left, then right, wings flapping and body off the ground, down with the claws outstretched for the kill. Retreat! But hard as he tried, Jose couldn't shake off the thought: *our* fighting cock.

Jose saw Adolfo slowly roll the sweet-smelling tobacco between his fingers. He had put the bird to bed in the crate at the back of the house and then squatted beside it. Jose watched the bird now as it moved about restlessly.

'People cut the comb on the bird because they believe it gives them better vision,' Adolfo said, and peered at the cigarette. A shaft of light from the room sloped out over the dark veranda. Satisfied that he had rolled his cigarette correctly, Adolfo lit a match, then puffed deeply. Jose thought about the fighting cocks and the fine pink line in the centre of their tiny heads. Evil, ugly, like devils. He couldn't imagine their bird having its comb cut.

'You're not going to cut its comb, are you Tio?' he asked anxiously.

'No, no, no!' Adolfo shook his head. 'To cut the bird is to rob it of its pride.' Then he looked at Jose and added, 'Without pride a fighter has no courage.'

14

No-Name Bird

As the weeks passed, Jose noticed a change in Adolfo. There was a strange sadness about his face and he seldom smiled. One morning as they were just about to start up the gravelled road as usual, Adolfo carrying the bird, Jose was aware that there was something peculiar about his uncle. Even though he had the bird in the crook of his arm and whispered soothing words down on it, something was missing. Then Jose realised: Adolfo wasn't carrying the pole with the net.

'Your pole, you've forgotten your pole!'

Adolfo kept walking.

'Tio? Do you want me to run back and get it?'

'No!' Adolfo said sharply.

'Tio?'

'I have no need for it any more.'

'Why not?'

Adolfo sighed. 'The tourists are all gone. The Chef de

Posto said that there was no more money for the pool. The Portuguese will leave soon.'

'But who will look after the pool?'

'There is no one.'

'But what about the new people, those who will take over Timor? Will they not look after the pool?'

'They are busy squabbling among themselves. It will take time.'

Later, after school, as Jose watched Adolfo work the bird, the silence around the pool was eerie. The pump that kept the water clean had stopped. On the third day, dark green scum floated in the corner of the pool. On the fifth day it began to smell.

Although the Portuguese officers and the Timorese soldiers were still about, Fretilin men and occasionally women now began to swagger about Baucau. They were dressed in camouflage jackets and trousers and caps with sun-flaps at the back, and they were carrying weapons. Jose knew many of the men; some were Baucau boys and had gone to his school and were only a few years older. He knew Angelo, Ricardo de Silva's brother.

Angelo had been at the school two years before and everyone knew what a good soccer player he was. Father Petri, who, people said, had been a soccer star in Portugal before he joined the priesthood, confirmed that Angelo was so good he could go to Lisbon to play for the big clubs. Now, dressed in his army uniform, he stood at the school gate smoking a cigarette, a rifle hanging from his shoulder. Like the others, Jose rushed towards him as soon as he was spotted.

Tall and gangly, Angelo had a way of laughing that made others laugh with him. Once he flipped back his head and showed his mouthful of fine white teeth, it was impossible not to be infected by his humour. He laughed as he answered the many questions about the gun. Hey Angelo! How many bullets can it shoot? How far can it shoot the bullets? Do you have other guns? Have you fired a cannon? Have you shot someone? Someone bad, perhaps?

With a quick flip of his fingers, Angelo showed them how to unload the gun. By working the bolt, the bullets fell to the red dirt, making small thud-thud-thud sounds. Jose clapped his hands. It looked so easy. Then Angelo showed them how to fire the gun. He placed one foot before the other and put the gun to his shoulder, closed one eye and squinted along the barrel, aiming it at the concrete ruins on the other side of the market square. Boom-boom-boom, he shouted. Everyone squealed with delight.

When he moved off, six of the boys lined up behind him and tried to march in step. Angelo kept turning his head, laughing. One-two-three-four, they yelled. He thought it was a great joke!

On the mornings before school, as Jose watched from the top of the stairway leading down to the pool, he saw Adolfo wet their bird's feathers and then tie it up on a long piece of string attached to a stake. The stake was out in the open and there was no shade for the bird most of the day. By the afternoon when Jose returned from school, the bird seemed distressed and was gasping for breath. Only then did Adolfo take it into his arms and allow it to drink from the pool. He would also throw it into the scummy water and make it swim about.

At night, after they had eaten, Adolfo prepared special food for the bird, chopping pieces of pork, and mixing it with yellow maize and enriched rice. He also sprinkled powdered sugar over the food. Jose helped, carefully grinding the sugar with a steel spoon and he brought fresh water in a can from the container in the kitchen. Sometimes Adolfo's eyes held his and he nodded. They understood each other's thoughts. Their bird was turning into a fighter.

'Our bird?' Jose asked.

Tio Adolfo smiled a rare smile. '*Our* bird!'

But it became a daily ritual for Carmillo and the others to stand above the pool and hurl pebbles. Every morning on the way to school the stones rained down, an act repeated in the late afternoon. Adolfo at first tried to take no notice but then, as soon as he saw Carmillo on the road above, he grabbed the bird and carried it to the far side of the pool where the stones couldn't reach.

A couple of times Jose turned and picked up a handful of pebbles and hurled them back at Carmillo.

Adolfo was angry. 'It's not a good thing to fight violence with violence.'

'But they could hurt the bird.'

'The bird is safe.'

The daily stone-throwing and yelling irritated Senhor Guido, the officer at the Baucau barracks and he ordered a soldier to appear on the parapet about the time Jose made a dash from school, ahead of Carmillo and his horde. The presence of the soldier put an end to the stone throwing and noise for a while, but soon he was needed elsewhere. He was marched back to the barracks, and Carmillo resumed his attack.

Everyone was concerned by the troubles. At school, Sister Philomena sighed a lot and one by one the class was gradually depleted. The Portuguese were the first; without fuss or bother, without saying goodbye, they simply failed to turn up at the morning assembly. Then most of the Chinese disappeared. Only Old Wong's grandson and two of his cousins remained.

Carmillo had an answer for everything. 'You too will run with the frightened birds.'

'I won't!' Jose came back at him.

'My father said you will leave for Portugal soon. You and your family will run like the rest!'

'We won't!' Jose said stubbornly, and left it at that.

Jose thought Adolfo happiest when he was working the bird, as there was now nothing for him to do around the pool. Gradually, the grass grew longer and then yellowed for lack of watering, and more green slime floated on the surface of the pool. Adolfo didn't seem to notice. The bird totally absorbed his interest.

If working with the bird during the day gave Adolfo strength and purpose, he was drained and listless in the evenings. Jose watched as his uncle sat at the table in the kitchen, head bowed, unhappy and dejected and hardly able to eat. Jose knew he only waited for the moment when he could put the bird to rest and creep into his own room. His stepfather Miguel seemed depressed too. He spent more and more time at Old Wong's store, drinking beer, talking about the troubles. It was now difficult to get trucks through to Ioro, on the very eastern tip of Timor. Old Wong had already lost a truck – a band of men stopped it, then simply pulled the driver off, beat him, and took off with the load.

'Why did the men take the truck?' Jose asked his stepfather.

'They said they needed it for the fighting.'

'The fighting again . . .' Jose began.

'Fretilin, UDT, who knows. Everyone is confused.'

'Perhaps they were only villagers who were hungry,' Adolfo said softly.

'Perhaps!' Miguel said and opened another bottle of beer.

Theresa had little patience with Miguel's beer-drinking. She came home from the hospital later and later and her news was more and more disturbing. There was fighting in the hills around Balibo and the troubles were spreading. 'We have four men with bad wounds at the hospital and all you two can do is drink beer and talk about cockfighting.'

Jose thought this was unfair. 'Adolfo doesn't drink beer, Mamma!' he said in defence.

His mother's stare chilled him to the bone. 'I don't want any smart talk.'

Because cooking was women's work, they had to wait until she came from the hospital before food was on the table. By this time, Jose's stomach was usually rumbling. Jose asked Theresa several times why she worked at the hospital such long hours. 'Because I'm needed,' she said simply.

Once when he asked, she fought back tears and said: 'I hope Senhor Jack and the Blonde Lady will come soon. Time is running out!'

Jose knew what that meant. 'I don't want to leave!' he said but it was as if she hadn't heard. She just pressed him against her belly and rocked him gently from side to side.

After they had eaten, Theresa went to bed straight away for she was so tired from the day at the hospital. Jose padded along the corridor and sat cross-legged on the soft-woven mat in Adolfo's room. Electricity was in spasmodic supply and Adolfo had already lit the lamp. Sensing there was danger, Adolfo had brought the bird's crate in from the yard and it rested now in the corner near his cot. Jose knew Adolfo feared the troubles would hurt the bird.

Jose wanted to ask about the fighting in the hills but Adolfo fended off any further talk with a flick of his hand. 'Fretilin are becoming strong. They are well organised.'

'They will take over from the Portuguese, Tio.'

'Perhaps. But there are other parties, UDT and Apodeti. Whenever you get a few people talking, they form another party. UDT want the Indonesians to have some say in Timor's independence, Apodeti want Timor to be Indonesian.'

'But you want Timor to be free, don't you Tio?'

'Yes. We must stand on our own feet!'

At the sound of their talking, the bird poked its beak through the wire mesh and blinked about. Its eyes sparkled in the yellow glow of the lamp.

Adolfo reached out and touched the fire-red comb.

Jose too began playing with it. The bird pecked gently at their fingers. 'What shall we call it, Tio? It must have a name!'

Adolfo raised himself from the cot and said in a firm, almost angry voice: 'It is a fighting cock. It has no name!'

The rejection hurt. 'It's such a beautiful bird. A great bird. A fighter. You said so yourself, Tio! What about Pedro for a name? Or Enrico? Or . . .'

'Stop, stop!' Adolfo shouted, holding up a hand. His head tumbled vigorously from side to side. 'No name, no name. It is only a bird. It is trained to fight and kill. It could be killed itself.'

Jose ignored Adolfo's words. He tried another way. 'What about a silly name? Like Peck-Peck? Or . . .'

Tio Adolfo's eyes rolled angrily. He flapped his hands about. 'No, *no*! It must not have a name. It's a *fighting* bird! It must not have a name.' He was on his feet beside the cot, pushing Jose firmly out of the room. 'It's time for you to go.'

No-Name Bird, that's it, Jose thought. That'll be its name. No-Name Bird. No-Name Bird.

Several times during the night he woke and heard strange crackling sounds, like the fireworks let off in front of Old Wong's store on Chinese New Year. Noise to drive away the evil spirits. But the sounds were a long way off. No-Name Bird, No-Name Bird, he mouthed silently. He put his head down and slept.

15

Carmillo

Doctor Manfredo listened carefully to the noises in Jose's chest through his stethoscope. Then he tapped Jose's back and felt around his neck and shoulders. When he had taken the instrument out of his ears he nodded. He looked down at Jose through thick glasses, which made the doctor's eyes seem enormous. 'You're a very healthy young man, Jose,' he said, then to Theresa, 'Very healthy!'

He smiled at Jose. 'There was your heart, your breathing, yes, a lot of noise. But all healthy noise!' He went to the side table and readied an injection. 'This is going to protect you, Jose.'

Jose watched the doctor insert the needle into a smaller bottle, then draw it out. He held the injection up against the light and sprayed some of the liquid into the air. 'This won't hurt.'

'No,' Jose said.

The needle punched into his arm. A tiny prick of pain

and it was all over. 'There,' the doctor said and smiled with yellow, tobacco-stained teeth. Jose watched the doctor write on a form, then stamp it with a large, round rubber seal, noting something in the little book his mother said was a passport. 'Your mother tells me you want to study law in Lisboa?' Doctor Manfredo said without looking up.

'Yes, Senhor. My uncle Carlo is an advocate.'

'An advocate, eh? A good profession.' He handed the documents to Theresa. 'Here you are, Senhora.' He pushed his glasses to the top of his head and rubbed at his eyes wearily. 'Difficult times, Senhora. Jose is one of the lucky ones.'

In the corridor outside there were several men with bloody bandages, lying on stretchers against the wall. One of them, a Timorese soldier, reached his hand towards Theresa. 'Help me, help me, please...' Army men were running along the corridor. Theresa held Jose's hand and pulled him along. 'Don't look, Jose, don't look,' she said tightly.

But he did look. He did look, and he saw pain and fear in the brown faces. He looked and he saw the stump of a leg covered with scarlet bandages. And further along he saw a man sitting on a stool, head held high with eyes hidden by white gauze.

His father had been a soldier. Is this what soldiers did? Fight and hurt each other. Gradually it came to him. As if a veil had been lifted from before his eyes. He saw the bloodied soldiers on the stretchers, he registered the pain and fear in their eyes, and he smelled the overpowering odour of torn bodies.

He began to shake, as if a chill had suddenly overcome him.

Outside, Theresa took several large breaths. 'You all right, Jose?' She touched his cheek with a fingertip. Then she pushed him from her. 'Jose, go to Adolfo. You saw the men back there. I must go back and help. Go and find your uncle.'

For a moment, Jose watched as she went back into the hospital, and then he began to run, run as fast as he could, towards the pool and Adolfo.

Adolfo squatted in the shade of the palm beside the pool and No-Name Bird pecked at the dirt between his feet. Occasionally, Adolfo would slap at the insects buzzing around his head. It was mid-afternoon.

'Adolfo... Adolfo...!' Jose said, out of breath. He wanted to tell him about the soldiers and the bloody bandages, the smell!

Adolfo peered up from under his hat and brushed a hand quickly over his mouth. 'Did the injection hurt?'

'No, but the men, the wounded men...' He gulped air.

'War is horror,' he said simply.

'Mamma is helping them...'

'Try not to think about the bad things, Jose. You will soon go to Lisboa to be with your uncle. Forget about what you have seen!' He started to roll a cigarette. 'It is best.' After he had finished the task, he lit a match. The smooth ritual of his actions calmed Jose. His breathing returned to normal. 'You will learn much in Lisboa. You will become a very important person.'

'I don't want to. I want to stay here with you, and Mamma, and Miguel, with No-Name Bird . . . I'll be all alone in Portugal.'

Just then, No-Name Bird raised his head and crowed. The sound broke the heaviness Jose felt in his chest. He brushed a hint of tears from his eyes. 'Will you work No-Name Bird this afternoon?'

Adolfo pushed the floppy hat down further over his eyes. 'No, no more work for the bird. It is ready.'

'Ready to fight?'

'Yes.'

They both watched the bird in silence. Then Carmillo appeared above on the parapet. He was alone.

Jose got up in expectation of the rain of stones, but Carmillo made no move. He stood on the stone railing, feet wide apart, hands on his hips, but instead of the usual stream of abuse there was nothing. He looked down at them a long time, then shrugged his shoulders and was gone.

Jose was again surprised next morning when he didn't see Carmillo and the others waiting in ambush on the road to the pool. In fact, as he walked along the gravelled road, with Adolfo carrying No-Name Bird, he was suspicious that Carmillo's absence was yet another trick to create a false sense of security. An ambush would come from some new hiding place. Adolfo too peered about as he walked, clutching the bird closely, ready to bolt at the first sign of danger. But Carmillo didn't appear. There was no one about.

Instead, Carmillo stood at the school gate with Luis and

Franco, waiting for Jose to arrive. Jose kept his eyes down, searching for something on the ground, but then Carmillo moved towards him. Jose realised he was in for a beating.

But Carmillo only turned and said simply: 'Will Adolfo fight the cock soon?'

'Oh, oh,' Jose said in surprise. He had expected something different and Carmillo had caught him off guard. 'He will fight!'

'The bird will not win,' Carmillo said in a serious, almost formal tone. 'My father says his birds are the best.'

'They were the best. Now there is another.'

A dark cloud crossed Carmillo's face. Jose thought the others would lash out and he tensed his body for a blow. But nothing happened. Carmillo, his fleshy crimson cheeks puffed out, shifted from one foot to the other as if he didn't know what to do. Then he shrugged. 'My father says the whole of Baucau is laughing at Adolfo. He is a fool training a cock from the hills.' Carmillo began to laugh, rocking his body to and fro, and the others too laughed.

Suddenly something burst in Jose. All he saw was a brilliant white flash before his eyes, searing and burning. Then he was on the ground and on top of Carmillo, every limb punching, kicking. Flat on the dust of the schoolyard, Jose realised instantly that Carmillo's big body was useless. It was all soft and spongy. Like a feather pillow, and Jose lashed out again and again.

A hand grabbed Jose by the back of the neck and pulled him upright. A meaty palm connected with the side of his head. Bright stars danced around him and the pain was bad. When he opened his eyes, he stared up into the black, angry face of Sister Philomena. 'Everyone's fighting! What's the matter with you all? People are fighting in the hills, they shoot at each other along the coast and even in the schoolyard I see people hurt each other. What's the *matter* with you all?' Without letting go of Jose's neck, she reached down and pulled up Carmillo. 'Now, no more fighting, you two, do you hear? No more fighting . . .' she yelled.

In the classroom, Sister Philomena carried on her lesson as if nothing had happened. Carmillo sat silently with the others, watching her every move. No one dared do anything out of place.

That afternoon after school, as Jose made his way along the gravelled road to the pool, Carmillo and his horde followed at a distance, a silent procession. Ever suspicious, Jose climbed down the stairs and pushed through the now knee-high grass towards Adolfo and No-Name Bird. He looked back several times, expecting a break-out of abuse and a storm of stones. But nothing happened.

Adolfo too was suspicious and had placed No-Name Bird on a dry sandy area among the once well-cut lawn on the far side of the pool. Toni the gardener had not been at the pool for over six weeks. Adolfo said that he had gone back to his family at Laga for there was no work at the Posada.

Adolfo looked towards the parapet and said: 'Why are they watching us like that? And in silence too?'

'I think they want to see No-Name Bird fight.'

'It does not have a name!'
'It's called No-Name Bird!'
'Just a fighting cock!'

Adolfo grumbled words Jose couldn't understand. Jose watched as his uncle went to No-Name Bird and untied it. He took it to the middle of the open space to the left of the pool and there with a rag put it through the motions of a fight. Shaping up, attack, retreat. Great shouts of 'ooohs' and 'aaahs' went up, so loud that soon a couple of the soldiers wandering by stopped to see what the noise was all about. Angelo too, in uniform and carrying his gun, joined the crowd. 'Heee-ii!' he yelled down at Adolfo and Jose, waving the gun triumphantly over his head.

16

Old Wong Considers a Request

Just a short distance from the school the gravelled road turned sharply. Jose saw Adolfo waiting at the top of the rise. He carried No-Name Bird in his arms and his floppy hat was pulled down over his eyes to protect against the hot afternoon sun.

Jose looked about for Carmillo. It was the third day that Carmillo had failed to appear.

'Come, we must see Old Wong,' Adolfo growled as he started up the road.

'Why do we have to see Old Wong?'

'Money! To bet on the bird.'

As they passed the Posada, Toni the gardener was sitting on one of the front steps, smoking clove-flavoured tobacco. His head hung low and his face was sad.

'Hey-eeei!' Adolfo shouted. 'How goes it today? Back from Laga so soon?'

Toni moved his head from side to side. He didn't look

up, just kept looking at the ground.

'No sweeping to keep you busy?'

'The Chef de Posto has gone. There is no money for the Posada. Everyone has left.'

Adolfo shrugged his shoulders.

'What about you? The pool is filthy!'

'The visitors will come to Timor again. It is all a matter of time.'

'The troubles will finish us all!'

'Take heart, Toni, take heart!'

Toni started to cackle, his body jerking as if possessed by the Unni-spirit.

Jose saw Old Wong warming his skinny body in the sun on the veranda of the general store. Miguel always said Old Wong was the richest man in Baucau.

'He-eeeh!' Old Wong shouted when he saw them come up the steps. 'You still carry the bird as though it was a babe.'

'It was my babe,' Adolfo said solemnly. 'Now it's my fighter.'

Jose pulled at Adolfo's shirt. '*Our* bird!'

'*Our* bird,' Adolfo whispered back.

Old Wong pulled his body up and squizzed intently at Adolfo, and then at the bird. His face broke into a grin, his teeth green and rotting.

'I want to match it on Sunday.'

'Ah!' The ancient Chinese hissed a long sigh. 'You wish me to give you money?'

Adolfo said nothing. He watched the bird in his arms.

Old Wong focused on Jose. 'What would people say of

Old Wong if they found out it was *his* money that was on a bird from up-country? Would they not say Old Wong was crazy? Crazy like some people who buy up-country cocks?' He paused a moment to regain his breath. He coughed, then recovered sufficiently to say: 'And besides, it's bad business to lend money. Especially in these times. It's only beginning. People are beating each other in your village, Adolfo, at Ermera. They say there has been shooting at Maliana.' He twitched, and shrugged. 'The bird would surely lose!'

Jose felt sad. Sad for Tio Adolfo. He lifted his head but saw that his uncle's face showed nothing. It was as if carved from black wood, like a Balinese statue.

That night, Jose saw Adolfo sit on his cot and it looked like a heavy load was pressing down on his uncle's body. No-Name Bird was in his arms.

As Jose sat with his back against the cool of the wall and watched silently, it seemed the bird felt Adolfo's hurt, for he made little whizzing sounds and snuggled close.

'I asked a lot of people for the money,' Adolfo said, barely above a whisper. 'I asked everyone . . .' and his voice trailed off as though it was difficult for him to speak.

'What will you do, Adolfo? Perhaps the bird should not fight.'

'The bird will fight, and it will win.'

'But there is no money for betting.'

'Something will come up. *I* only have a few escudos.'

The next afternoon was particularly hot and humid and Jose and Adolfo dozed under the palm at the far side of the pool. The smell from the pool was bad and Jose tried to ignore it. No-Name Bird pecked the ground in the shade.

Jose had just about dozed right off when he heard movement behind him. He blinked and tried to see. The glare was too bright, so he shielded his eyes. The bulky figure was unmistakable. 'Senhor Jack!' he said and jumped up.

The big man shook hands with them both. He was red from the heat and wet from the humidity.

Adolfo's face cracked in a wide smile. It was the first time Jose had seen his uncle smile in days. 'Ah, Senhor, you're back.'

Senhor Jack scratched his belly. 'We're all packed up, closing the drill in the south. Everyone's moving back to Australia. Well, for the time being anyway. Even though the fighting's stopped. Since UDT and Apodeti leaders, and some of their followers, have gone over the border into Indonesia . . .'

'Why would they do that, Senhor Jack?' Jose asked. His heart was beating mightily.

'The talk is that they want to declare independence and union with Indonesia.'

Adolfo pulled at his hat. 'They cannot do that! Fretilin won't allow it. They are strong fighters.'

'Well, it seems they have done it.'

'Then there will be more fighting, Senhor Jack . . .' Jose added.

'That is bad, Senhor,' Adolfo said. 'We do not want the Indonesians.'

'At least the fighting has stopped. Between the Timorese anyway. For the moment!'

'That is good news!' Jose thought a moment. 'And the Portuguese? Have they all gone? They have certainly left Baucau.'

'Yep, they've gone all right. Seems the government just packed up and shipped out. The ships, apparently, are waiting at Atauro?'

Adolfo lifted his head and laughed. 'The island of the goats!'

'Is that what it's called. Very appropriate!'

'Why are they waiting at Atauro, Senhor Jack?' Jose asked, puzzled.

'For the final word from Portugal to pull out. Everyone's waiting. God, what an atmosphere!' Senhor Jack scratched his stomach again. 'We're flying home next week. It's all over for us.' He turned to Jose. 'Judy is in Dili. She'll be back in Baucau by the weekend.'

Jose's heart missed a beat. He knew what it meant. Portugal.

Senhor Jack paused, then reached out and touched No-Name Bird. 'How's our cock? Eh? Has it had a fight yet?'

'On Sunday,' Adolfo said.

'Sunday? Think he's ready for it?'

'Oh yes, Senhor Jack, yes!'

Senhor Jack bent down and looked closely at No-Name Bird. 'Do you think it'll have a chance?'

Adolfo grunted.

'Tell you what. I might just come down and watch the fight on Sunday, eh? After all, I've got a sort of interest in the action, haven't I? Eh?'

It suddenly occurred to Jose – the solution to Adolfo's problem. 'Will you be betting, Senhor Jack?'

'Betting? Huh! Well, of course I'll put some money on the cock. That's half the fun, isn't it?'

Adolfo shot a glance across to Jose. There was a glint in his eyes.

Senhor Jack looked at his watch. 'God, I'd love a swim.' He turned to the pool and saw the scum floating on top. He rubbed at his nose. 'What a stink!' Turning, he clapped Adolfo on the shoulder. 'I've got to go.' He shrugged. 'They've fixed up a room for Judy and me at the Posada. One of Old Wong's sons has taken it over. At least the beer is cold. Apparently the generator at the back is still working. For now.'

'Yes, Senhor Jack.'

'Say, Adolf? Does the cock have a name? Do they give these birds a name?'

Adolfo moved his head. 'No name, Senhor Jack. Only a cock from up-country. From Bobonaro.'

No-Name Bird, No-Name Bird! Jose wanted to shout.

17

The Challenge

Jose didn't know if he slept or just moved from one dream to the other. Images played out before his eyes, people laughed, cried, his mother was there, also Miguel and Adolfo. A cockfight had already begun and it ended with Adolfo carrying No-Name Bird from the ring in triumph. The Chef de Posto attended too, as did Sister Philomena and Father Petri. The Portuguese officers and Timorese soldiers were laughing. Sister Philomena was taking away the books under his desk. You're going to Portugal; you don't need them any more, she said. No-Name Bird! No-Name Bird was going to fight today.

In the excitement of his half-dream his legs twitched, crossed and uncrossed in the humid night. He was covered with sweat.

Jose couldn't bear it any longer. He got up from the narrow cot and dressed in his khaki shorts, padded along the corridor to his uncle's room. Adolfo was still asleep, his mouth slightly open and emitting soft wheezing sounds. No-Name Bird popped his head through the mesh and blinked. Jose sat down in the corner against the wall and No-Name Bird watched intently, his tiny head moving from side to side.

From his pocket Jose took the rosary, the beads carved from red stone, a present from Father Petri for service as an altar boy. Slowly, holding the tiny marbles between index finger and thumb, he began to count off the prayers. *Don't suffer, little bird, No-Name Bird, be strong, courageous, brave . . .*

Jose didn't know how long he'd sat in the corner praying but as the grey light of dawn penetrated the room, Tio Adolfo stirred. Adolfo reached out and touched No-Name Bird, as if to reassure himself of his presence. He rubbed his eyes but didn't seem surprised that Jose was there.

'You didn't sleep much?'

Jose shook his head.

Adolfo put his feet down on the floor, searching for his sandals. 'I feel strong today, Jose, strong. Do you feel that strength?'

Jose nodded. He didn't feel strength; he was afraid of what the day would bring.

'The bird must feel strong!'

He reached out for No-Name Bird, pushing back the mesh and lifting the bird up and out of the crate. Then he pressed him to his naked chest.

From the slant of the light through the door, Jose knew it was time for church. 'I'm going to be late for mass,' he whispered. He had to hurry.

Adolfo continued to cradle No-Name Bird, crooning soft, strong words.

When Jose arrived at the market after mass, the fights had already started. He looked about for Adolfo. There! There was the floppy hat, on the far side of the crowd. It stood out from the blur of dark faces. Adolfo was sitting against the wall of the market building, No-Name Bird between his ankles. He squinted up as Jose appeared before him.

'Senhor Jack and the Senhora are back!' he said.

'Where, Tio?'

'I saw them by the pool earlier. The Senhora asked after you.'

Jose shuddered, as if chilled.

No-Name Bird blinked about nervously. Adolfo stroked the blood-red comb under his beak, and the action seemed to calm him.

As it was not his place to sit with an adult, Jose stood beside his uncle and watched. Once in a while, one of the men walked past with a cock in his arms and looked down at Adolfo. Jose could almost feel the contempt. Most of the birds were from Rikki's stable, fine big birds with strong legs and backs, pink cut combs and white feathers. No-Name Bird nestled between Adolfo's legs and Jose's lips trembled in fear. No-Name Bird seemed so small, so defenceless.

None of the men stopped to throw down a challenge; no one paused to stroke No-Name Bird and praise his strength. Nor even ridicule! Nothing. That was the worst part. Jose began to despair. Perhaps no one would challenge Adolfo. What would happen then?

The situation changed quickly when Senhor Jack arrived.

He pushed his way towards them, head and shoulders taller than the Timorese, the Chinese and the few Fretilin soldiers who had drifted up from the barracks to watch the fights, though more out of boredom than real interest. Senhor Jack was dressed in white slacks and a colourful shirt decorated with bright flowers. Jose looked about for the Blonde Lady. He desperately wanted her to be present.

'Hi-ya, Adolf. Got a fight yet?'

'No, not yet, Senhor Jack. But soon.'

'And Jose! Ready for the big trip?'

A lump hurt Jose's throat. Despite the feelings raging inside, he nodded. He didn't want to think about the journey.

'Bird all in shape?'

'Yes, Senhor.'

'What say, Adolf? Put a few hundred escudos on the bird?' He pulled a wad of notes from his pocket. Jose had never seen so many in a roll. 'Here, Adolf, we'll split fifty-fifty, eh?'

As Senhor Jack handed Tio Adolfo the money, a loud wail went up from the crowd gathered around them. Aee-ie! Aee-ie! That was *too* much money to place on an up-country bird!

Senhor Jack said he was going to walk around the half-built market building. 'You get yourself a match, Adolf, and I'll come and be your cheer squad.' He laughed loudly, then bent clumsily and stroked No-Name Bird's head. Instantly, the bird's collar of feathers flared and his comb rose in all its splendour. Adolfo held him tight; the bird would have launched an attack.

Another loud shout went up from the crowd. He had spirit, this up-country cock! Jose straightened his back. There was pride in his chest. After all, the bird belonged to him too!

The crowd seemed to want to trample over them in their sudden excitement at the bird's display of spirit. The men sensed there was something unusual in the air. Something was happening. What? What? A loud shout! The ring of men around Adolfo and Jose parted. Rikki, accompanied by an acne-scarred Chinese-Timorese man carrying a white bird, stalked into the circle. Jose saw Carmillo's bulky body behind his father.

'So this is the cock, the coward from up-country?' Rikki spat a stream of betel juice in front of Adolfo. 'So this is the cock you want to fight!'

Adolfo didn't move, but kept his eyes firmly on No-Name Bird.

'You want a match? Against mine?' Rikki's own words made him angrier. He shouted: 'Against my best? Eh, Adolfo? You want the shame of defeat against one of my beauties?' Another load of betel juice went splat in the dust.

Unlike Adolfo, Jose had his head high and was watching Rikki and Carmillo. It occurred to him that Rikki had doubts about his birds. It was No-Name Bird who looked the better fighter. That's why Rikki was shouting so much.

Rikki scowled around the circle, expecting others to take up his anger and indignation, but the men held their silence and watched. Only Carmillo sniggered loudly.

Sensing he would lose the crowd, Rikki snatched the cock from the Timorese-Chinese man and threw it to the ground in front of Adolfo. Jose gasped. It was a magnificent creature: big, white, with a pink comb shaven to make it look vicious and mean. As soon as it spied No-Name Bird its neck twitched, the collar feathers came up like a brush and the cropped wings spread wide. Rikki reached down and held it tight. No-Name Bird waited patiently, almost serenely, blinking, safe and guarded between Adolfo's knees.

This time there rose a long, drawn-out wail of admiration and Rikki knew he had the crowd. He scooped up the bird and pushed it back into the arms of the Timorese-Chinese man, then, rudely pointing a finger into Adolfo's face, he shouted: 'See, he's mad, mad, mad!' At that, the crowd erupted in a storm of laughter and betel juice hit the hard-trampled dirt in front of Adolfo like splashes of rain.

Slowly, deliberately, taking full advantage of the moment, Adolfo took from his pocket the notes Senhor Jack had given him and placed them in a neat pile on the ground before No-Name Bird. The laughter died.

Rikki did a nervous, comical skip, then slammed his own handful of notes down on top of the pile of money. He turned, too quickly, for he collided with Carmillo. Rikki raised his hand and elbowed his son roughly out of the way, then pushed towards the rim of the circle. One of the Chinese bookies hovering to one side took up the notes and stuffed them into his already bulging pockets.

The crowd broke up. The men began to bet. Jose looked about, a little startled by all the activity. Carmillo, head down, lingered a moment, then spat in Jose's direction.

18

The First Round

Jose learnt that the cocks are not fought in the ring by their owners but by professional matchmakers. So as soon as the fight details had been settled, Adolfo was approached by a couple of matchmakers who wanted to give service, but he shook his head and finally chose Mateo, the Goa-born head waiter at the Posada.

'Mateo! Mateo!' Jose shouted, trying to catch the man's attention. He knew him well. His son Alfonso was a classmate.

'Is the bird ready?' Mateo asked.

'Yes,' Jose heard himself say in unison with Adolfo.

Mateo spoke quickly with Adolfo, settling the fee. Then he squatted in front of Adolfo and examined No-Name Bird carefully. He felt around his legs, the wings, and with two fingers he prised open the beak to see if there was any obstruction. He nodded his approval. From his back pocket he pulled out a leather case. While Adolfo held the bird, Mateo selected a steel spur from the five blades in the case, cushioned on green velvet. Double-edged, eight centimetre blades: one end sharp and cruel, the other filed blunt to enable it to be tied to the bird's left foot. Expertly, with a green thread, Mateo wrapped the blade along the natural spur to give it extra strength, the sharp end jutting backwards.

A thin wail of excitement went up from the crowd. A small group had decided to back No-Name Bird, and murmuring amongst themselves they clustered to one side. On the far side of the ring, Rikki and his supporters grouped around the white Baucau bird. There was much laughter.

Mateo cupped his hands around the body of No-Name Bird and taking care to keep the blade away from his chest, placed him on the ground to let him get his balance. Then quickly, he snatched away his hand. For a moment No-Name Bird stood still, blinking up at the men towering over him. But like a dancer, Jose thought, he moved his right foot, then the left with the spur. Testing the ground. A couple of times he strode up and down in the narrow confines that the crowd allowed.

It was now late afternoon and the market building cast a long shadow over the ring. Because Mateo arrived first he chose to stand with his back to the sun. He and Adolfo squatted down, Jose immediately behind them, while their supporters grouped themselves around. Suddenly, there she was. The Blonde Lady with Senhor Jack. Jose waved frantically. 'Come this way, Lady, please, please!' he shouted. She returned his wave but her face was drawn and unhappy.

As they came closer, Jose yelled excitedly: 'No-Name Bird is fighting. He-iiih!'

The Blonde Lady wiped her face with a white handkerchief.

'You give it to them, Adolfo,' Senhor Jack said in his gruff voice, puffing on a cigar. 'Eh? Give them hell!'

'I don't think I'll watch,' the Blonde Lady said. Her voice was almost like a cry.

'Senhora, Senhora, please stand here . . .' Jose wanted her to have a good position so she could see No-Name Bird fight. But she turned her head away.

Senhor Jack was angry. 'You watch it, Judy. You'll never have a chance like this again.'

A roar went up from Rikki's side. His matcher lifted the Baucau cock high above his head to carry it into the ring and the crowd followed in a tight-packed body. They spread out on either side of the ring, elbowing each other to get a good position.

A hush came over them. Only Mateo and the other man were now in the ring. Holding the birds cupped in their hands before them, they slowly walked to the centre of the ring and when they were almost toe to toe, with one brisk movement as if it had been rehearsed, they brought the birds up, the heads just touching. Three times they swooped the birds above their heads. In the last arc, without breaking the rhythm, the cocks were placed down on the hard-packed red earth, held an instant to allow them to get their balance, and then let go. As Mateo stepped back to the edge of the ring, it was the combless white Baucau cock which attacked first.

It ran a circle around No-Name Bird, then lurched itself forwards, its white wings outstretched. It lifted itself a full half-metre above, then stalled, with claws up and the knife flashing vertically. Jose clearly heard the thud as the bird landed on top of No-Name Bird. A high-pitched, hysterical sound rose over the crowd as No-Name Bird staggered around the ring, his brown and black feathers stained crimson. Rikki's man held the Baucau bird high as though in victory and a couple of supporters jumped into the ring and danced madly about.

Expertly, Mateo examined No-Name Bird.

Adolfo was on his feet. 'The feather, the feather. Give it the feather!' he shouted when he saw the bird gasp for breath.

Mateo nodded and with a quick flick of his wrist, he plucked out one of No-Name Bird's tail feathers. Holding the bird under one arm, he prised open his beak again and with thumb and forefinger he rammed the feather down, point first. Several times he pumped it up and down. It restored No-Name Bird's wind. The bird moved his head about in quick, jerky movements, then breathed normally.

'Oh!' the Blonde Lady cried. 'I can't stand any more of this, Jack. I'm going!'

He tried to restrain her, holding her arm. 'But the bird's going to fight again.'

'I don't care, Jack, I just don't care.' She tried to push through the crowd. The circle, however, was tightly packed and she had trouble getting through.

Jose wanted to pull her back. No-Name Bird will win! he shouted silently.

Out in the ring, the men were still dancing hysterically, but Rikki and his matcher sat on the far side, watching, waiting for Mateo to bring No-Name Bird back into the fight.

Mateo quickly tested the green wool binding around the bird's spur, then stood up and with a yell, came to the centre of the ring.

19

The Blonde Lady is Angry

If Jose thought No-Name Bird was hurt, it was for no more than an instant, for this time the bird didn't wait for the other to make the first move, but attacked immediately. With his neck feathers flaring, he rushed to the left of the other bird, just as Adolfo had trained him to do. Then with a wingspan between them he turned, spreading his feathers, the red comb over his beak like a bloodied flag. His strong wings and light body carried him higher than the other bird. When he stalled, claws out, the knife was almost vertical above the other bird's back. Down it came on the wing, cutting deep. Jose let out a cry as he saw the Baucau cock stumble, crow weakly, and with an effort, fly up against the other. But it had left the move too late. No-Name Bird was already above it, not high this time but still above. Down swooped the knife, cruel in a vicious arc, pricking the other's neck.

What had been a murmur from the crowd before was now wild and excited yelling.

Again and for the third time the birds came together in mid-air. They were tired now and both had lost blood, too tired to lift their bodies up. The knives cut low and from the side. As the birds drew apart, there was a shower of tiny feathers. For no more than an instant the birds stood perfectly still, eyes blinking, gasping for breath, but then No-Name Bird with one last desperate lunge, spread his wings and lifted himself up off the ground.

And the blade came down.

Mateo snatched No-Name Bird and held him high. His cry was almost simultaneous with the Blonde Lady's. Hers was a high-pitched, thin sound. It stunned the crowd to silence.

She was close to Jose and he heard her clearly. 'You're savages!'

Senhor Jack turned to her just as the man at her side received a hard whack on the chest. He tumbled backwards and was saved from falling only by the dense wall of bodies. Senhor Jack, moving quickly, clamped his arms around her. He led her across the empty marketplace, then up the stairway to the gravelled road above.

Jose turned. All eyes, white discs in dark faces, were following Senhor Jack and the Blonde Lady. No one moved; all was silent. Then it was Mateo, standing in the middle of the ring with No-Name Bird held high on one arm, blood running down his forearm in a thick red line, who broke the crowd's spell. His shout was an eerie sound: loud and clear. At his feet the Baucau bird with its white feathers spotted scarlet made one attempt to get up but it stumbled and lay still, eyes wide, beak gasping for air.

Mateo yelled something to Adolfo. But Adolfo shook his head and pointed towards Jose.

Mateo nodded. He took two steps across the ring and handed Jose the bird.

Jose's throat choked. He took the bird, gently, conscious of his injuries, pressing the hot-feathered body close. *No-Name Bird is mine!* He was oblivious of the noise around him.

'Adolfo . . .' Jose began.

Adolfo nodded.

The bird was his. He held him in his arms and looked down at the tiny head. He pecked at Jose's arm.

The men were in the ring now, a thick, black, brown and yellow, sweating, dusty, jumping, dancing mass, with Adolfo in the middle. He had lost his floppy hat and his face, neck and torso were glistening.

Jose glanced up just in time to see Carmillo at the side of the ring, his usually pink-flushed face drained of colour. His chin rested on his chest and the corners of his mouth were pulled down. He looked up. Jose would never forget Carmillo's haunting, hurt eyes.

Jose sat down in the shade of the large jacaranda tree, arms outstretched, elbows resting on his knees just like Tio Adolfo would squat, and between his thighs was No-Name Bird. He had tucked his feet under his wings and though his head was high and occasionally he would shake his comb, he breathed with great difficulty. Jose glanced up. Adolfo stood over him, his body outlined in streaks of gold from the sinking sun.

'He should have had a name,' Jose said, half in anger, half sorrow. 'He should have had a grand name, a beautiful name, a name of honour.'

Adolfo moved down beside him. 'Birds have no names,' he said gently. 'Men and women have names, not fighting cocks. Their courage is enough. They are known for their courage, not their names.'

'His name is No-Name Bird,' Jose said stubbornly.

Tio Adolfo reached out and touched Jose's shoulder. His hand felt warm and soothing. 'It is a fitting name.'

They sat side by side for some time. Once in a while, one of the men would pass on the way to drink at the stream and would look down at them and nod. Adolfo took from a small leather pouch the crumpled notes he had won and straightened them as best he could, then made two piles, folding each carefully.

'This is for Portugal,' he said and pointed at one of the piles. 'The other is Senhor Jack's.'

'For Portugal?' Jose felt as though he was sitting in a mist. 'Why Portugal?'

'It will help you on your trip.'

'Portugal.' Jose spoke the word but the voice was not his own.

'We must go,' Adolfo said finally and stood up. He mumbled something about having to give Senhor Jack his money, and as he made his way across the now deserted cockpit and marketplace, Jose stumbled after him, still holding No-Name Bird tight. His thoughts were racing. I will make a comfortable bed for No-Name Bird, make sure he gets the best food, cool water to drink, warmth so that his wounds heal. He is *my* bird now!

There was no one about at the Posada. Usually on Sundays the inn would be a centre of activity with tourists, Portuguese officers and their wives. But only Toni the gardener stood by the main entrance now, half of his body in the shadow, like a soldier on guard.

'They've all gone. All gone! Everyone's gone to Dili!' His toothless mouth was a black hole in his face. His eyes moved quickly from Adolfo to Jose to No-Name Bird. 'You've come to give me the bird for soup?'

'We give you nothing! We're here to speak to Senhor Jack,' Adolfo said. He held out the crumpled escudo notes. 'This belongs to Senhor Jack.'

Toni grinned. 'Escudos are worthless now.'

'They belong to Senhor Jack!'

Toni peered down at No-Name Bird. 'You can't bring it into the Posada. No animals allowed.'

'If the Portuguese are all gone, who cares?'

'It is not permitted.'

'Jose can wait here with the bird.'

Toni considered. 'He must stay here, and not move.'

'He will do this!'

'Then come, Adolfo. I'll show you Senhor Jack's room!'

As the two men disappeared into the dark interior of the inn, Jose slowly moved up the stone steps until he stood at the huge, wide-open wooden door. Gradually his eyes adjusted to the gloom beyond. He placed one foot carefully before the other, holding the bird tight, and the

Posada enfolded him. He had never been inside before and he marvelled at how cool it was, and everything so wide and spacious! The corridor was wide enough for four men to walk down it, side by side.

Adolfo stood with Toni at one of the doors about halfway down the corridor. Jose could just make out Senhor Jack's head jutting out, the light behind him. He seemed very angry, shouting at Adolfo. Tio Adolfo's arm was outstretched holding the money. But Senhor Jack pushed his hand away.

From inside the room Jose heard the Blonde Lady – a low moan. Then Jose saw Senhor Jack grab Adolfo by the shoulder and give him a shove, propelling him up the corridor towards him. They nearly collided for the force of the push had been so strong, but just as Jose twisted to the side to protect the bird, his uncle smashed against the wall. Toni stepped forward to help. And Senhor Jack slammed shut the door.

20

Under Fire

Adolfo helped Jose shift the crate to his room and after they had washed the bird's wounds with salt and water, they watched him settle. He took naturally to his new surrounds, snuggling amongst the rags, pecking affectionately at Jose's fingers.

'It knows its new master!' Adolfo said approvingly.

After his uncle went to bed, Jose stretched out on the cot and watched the bird for a long time. His mind was a jumble of ideas and plans about what he would do with the bird – prepare special feed for him, take him for workouts beside the pool, even show him off in the schoolyard. That is, if Sister Philomena approved. Everyone will know that Jose and No-Name Bird are friends.

In the morning, it was Jose who carried the bird along the gravelled road. As they walked, the bird soft and warm against his chest, Jose was quite aware of how uneasy his uncle felt without his pole and net. They had been his badge of office. Now he had no pool to clean. He had even given away his bird. He wanted desperately to say something to Adolfo, but the pride and pleasure of having the bird in his arms was overpowering. Only when they had reached the steps that led down to the pool did Jose turn to his uncle and hand him the bird.

One evening, over the dinner table, Miguel announced that there were no more driving jobs. After the last run, to Tutuala and Ioro on the very western tip of the island, Old Wong said it was the last delivery. 'He was more concerned about the truck than me!' Miguel said, sipping his beer. Jose felt troubled, and thought of Portugal.

'Did they shoot at the truck?' Jose asked at last.

'No, but Old Wong is afraid someone will steal it. And the cargo!'

'So there is fighting in the west, too.'

'No, Jose.' Miguel shook his head. 'But everyone is afraid.'

'Fretilin are fighting in the hills. The fighting will spread,' Adolfo added. 'I heard it on the radio.'

'The radio from Australia, Tio?'

'Yes.'

With the loss of his job, Miguel spent most of his time in the house, wandering about moodily, drinking his beer. When Jose came home from spending time with Adolfo at the pool, working No-Name Bird in an imaginary fight, he found his stepfather in the kitchen, flipping the dial of the transistor radio for the Bahasa Indonesian broadcast from Radio Australia. He was very interested in what was being said on the radio. In the evenings he sat listless at the table, his giant arms folded, eyes dull, sadness in the slope of his shoulders. There was always a bottle of beer at his elbow.

Theresa had no time for his moods. Each morning she left for the hospital just as dawn was breaking and she never returned until after dark. At first, as she prepared the meal, her talk was about the activities at the hospital: the wounded men they brought in from the hills, the fighting. But as the days passed Jose was all too aware of the change. Now she never talked as she prepared the food, she complained constantly about being tired, there were blue shadows under her eyes and her shoulders curved in a hunch. Once, when she came home very late and was exhausted, it was Adolfo who took over the cooking. Theresa just sat in the chair, unable to move, her legs propped high on a cushion. She cried because she was so tired. She cried because Adolfo cooked – women's business. From that night onwards, it was Adolfo who prepared the evening meal.

Tonight Theresa glared at Miguel and his bottle of beer and there was a disapproving curl on her lips. 'There must be *something* you can do other than sit around the house and drink beer,' she said abnormally softly.

Miguel shrugged his shoulder.

'Doesn't Old Wong have something for you to do? Help out in the store? Shift things around in the storeroom?'

Miguel sipped from the bottle.

'Adolfo still helps out at the pool!'

Jose looked across at his uncle. Tio Adolfo moved his head slightly. Jose knew that there was no work for

Adolfo to do. He spent most of the day working the bird with the glove and talking to Toni the gardener who also didn't have a job.

After they had finished eating and Theresa had gone to bed, Jose helped clear the pots and plates off the table, making sure that any leftovers were saved for No-Name Bird.

Miguel and Adolfo spent a lot of time listening to the radio. Both understood Bahasa Indonesian and Adolfo also made an effort to understand the English broadcast. Occasionally, one of them would look up and shake his head. 'There is a lot of bloodshed,' Adolfo said sadly. 'It is terrible when our own people fight each other.'

One evening, about a week after Senhor Jack and the Blonde Lady had flown back to Dili on the oil company aircraft, there was loud knocking on the beam above the door. Miguel went out to look and then ushered in Henri da Costa, the orderly at the hospital. He was dressed in his uniform of khaki shorts and shirt. His eyes roved nervously about the room, looking first at Miguel, then Adolfo and finally Jose. In his hand he held a note from Doctor Manfredo. 'It's started, it's started,' Henri da Costa said over and over.

'What's started?' Jose asked.

'The fighting. UDT. They've taken the police station and airport at Dili. There is much shooting. And Baucau airport is closed.'

Theresa snatched the note from da Costa's hand. Her eyes raced over the lines, knuckles pressed to her lips. 'It's a message from Senhor Jack!' She glanced over at Jose and from her eyes he knew it concerned him. 'Oh Jose, Jose!' she said, and tears trickled down her cheeks. 'They're just waiting for a break to come and pick you up. They'll let us know.'

Jose sat at the table, unable to move. He heard his thumping heart and a voice inside his head screaming. What will become of No-Name Bird if I go? Who will take care of him? He will *die* without me!

Theresa stared at the note a long time, then wiped the tears from her eyes with a determined sweep of her hand. Suddenly aware that Henri da Costa was still standing uneasily in the doorway, she said: 'Thank you for bringing the message. Tell Doctor Manfredo it was kind of him to send you down.'

The orderly nodded and left.

Then, with a cry, she was beside Jose and had her arms tightly around him, pressing his head against her warm belly. 'Oh my Jose, Jose, Jose,' she said, crushing him to her body.

After what felt like a long time to Jose, she sighed and pushed him from her. He lifted his head to her tear-streaked face. 'Mamma . . .' he said and it was as if his heart would break.

'We have to pack, Jose, pack so that you're ready when they come for you.' She took his arm and pulled him to the bedroom. Jose thought how warm her hand was.

No-Name Bird pushed his head through the mesh as they came in. For a moment, Jose thought his mother would be angry at finding the bird in his room but for her the bird didn't exist. 'Wait here,' she said crisply. Then she was back with an army-issue rucksack. 'It was your father's.' The task of pulling shorts and shirts from the cupboard triggered a new flood of tears. One by one, she carefully folded the white shirts, the shorts, socks, and an extra pair of sandals. There was also a leather envelope containing his documents. 'You must *always* make sure you keep them somewhere *safe*,' she said emphatically.

Jose stood against the wall, mute, watching, pain in his belly. He kept glancing at No-Name Bird. What will happen to him? Who will feed him? Take care of him?

Theresa straightened and pushed the rucksack into the corner beside the bed. Large silvery beads rolled down her flushed cheeks and splashed on the cot, spreading to dark spots. She reached out and touched Jose's cheek. 'You won't forget your Mamma, will you? Ever? Even when you're famous, a Very Important Person.'

Jose threw himself into his mother's arms, feeling the soft warmth of her, the comfort, the security. Her arms came about him and she hugged him close. He never, ever wanted to leave that embrace.

Sometime during the night, Jose woke suddenly to the sounds of shots. Like firecrackers let off at Old Wong's store to celebrate Chinese New Year. Jose rubbed his eyes and looked out of the narrow window high up on the wall. There wasn't much to see except the silhouettes of the other houses. He turned and glanced at the crate by his bed. No-Name Bird had his head out, blinking about.

'It's nothing, nothing,' Tio Adolfo said from the doorway. 'Go back to sleep.'

'Are they shooting?'

'Yes. But it's at the back of the marketplace.'

Jose tried to sleep but couldn't. Too many thoughts raced about his head.

Next morning, Jose saw his first dead person.

As they came down the gravelled road, there was a crowd to one side of the stairway, watching something down below at the pool. Toni the gardener stood by the parapet and pointed. 'They shot him during the night.'

Jose peered over the edge. He shifted No-Name Bird onto his hip so he could get a better look. A man in army uniform, legs twisted under him, was lying on the grass near the edge of the pool. His head was cocked unnaturally to one side. The grass near the body was crimson.

'Angelo de Silva,' Adolfo said at his side. There was sadness in his voice.

'His mother hasn't been told,' someone said.

Jose felt sick. Angelo. 'I know his mother,' was all he could think of to say. 'She used to come to school. I . . . remember her.'

'It is a sad day for her.'

Three men slowly climbed down the stairway and walked across to the body. They stood over it, hands flapping as they talked. Then a Timorese soldier appeared with a blanket: he'd been a sergeant at the barracks with the Portuguese but was now Fretilin. He pushed his way through the crowd to join the men below.

The blanket was thrown over Angelo's twisted form but before his bloodied face was covered, Jose saw clearly the hordes of flies.

'I'll come with you as far as the school,' Tio Adolfo

said. As they walked, their sandals crunched on the gravel, and they heard an occasional pop-pop-pop-pop from the direction of Mata Bien.

'Shooting,' Jose said.

Adolfo had stopped and was listening intently. 'Yes, we'd better go quickly!'

A Fretilin soldier stood in front of the school gate when they got there, his rifle in the crook of his arm. He was shouting at the women and children. 'Go home, everyone go home. The school is closed. Go home!'

'Come, quickly,' Tio Adolfo said, his voice suddenly tinged with urgency.

They hurried back along the gravelled road and when they passed the stone parapet, Jose looked over the edge and saw that Angelo's body had gone. There was a dark patch where it had been.

Soldiers were running towards them. 'Get off the road!' one of them shouted.

Adolfo pulled Jose into the bushes. No-Name Bird let out a squawk as Jose clutched him tighter. He thought: this is where Carmillo and the others usually wait for us.

The soldiers were yelling, and then the shooting started. Pop-pop-pop-pop! The air whistled above their heads.

'*Down!*' Tio Adolfo said and pushed Jose's head to the ground. No-Name Bird struggled in his arms, kicking his legs, but Jose held firm. Then the earth shuddered with explosions.

'Mortars!' Adolfo whispered.

No-Name Bird thrashed about in mad panic. 'Hold it, hold it tight!' Adolfo said.

But just as suddenly as it had begun, the shooting and shouting stopped. There was only an isolated pop-pop-pop-pop on the far side of the marketplace now.

'Adolfo?'

'Shhh . . . stay *down!*'

A long time later, Adolfo finally stood up and looked about. 'Let's go quickly!'

But as they ran along the gravelled road, shooting again broke out behind them.

21

Trying to Find Safety

Miguel huddled over the table in the kitchen, holding his head. He was shaking visibly. 'The shooting, the shooting,' he said, over and over.

Tio Adolfo took charge and told Jose to place No-Name Bird in the crate in his room.

'I will hold him, Tio.'

'It is best,' he said in a stern, authoritative voice. 'Now help me!'

The three of them put the house's only high wardrobe, the one from the main bedroom, across the front door. The back room too was secured and the bamboo blinds pulled down over the windows. Everything was bathed in a curious half-light and it became very hot. Their faces glistened with perspiration.

'They'll break in!' Jose said.

Adolfo shook his head. 'Only if they're desperate to come in. They'll have to break the door and then the wardrobe.' He still had on his floppy hat, jammed tight on his head. 'Miguel, have a look in the kitchen. How much food and water is there?'

Miguel shuffled off, his sandals making scraping noises on the matting. From his unsteady movements, Jose thought he had already drunk a lot of beer.

'Will they come and kill us, Tio Adolfo?' Jose asked nervously, wanting to sound more curious instead of scared.

'No, we are nothing to them. They only want to kill each other.'

'Mamma!' It suddenly came to him that his mother was still up at the hospital.

Adolfo read his thoughts. 'She is safer there than here!'

Adolfo sank down with his back to the wall in the corridor and slowly began to roll a cigarette. 'We must wait until they have finished their fighting.'

Miguel returned from the kitchen and said there was plenty of food. 'For at least a week.' But the water was a problem. There were only a couple of containers with wash-up water, and one big plastic bottle suitable for drinking. 'And the beer!' Adolfo said, lighting his cigarette.

'And we have a transistor.' Miguel held up the small black radio. 'I only changed the batteries yesterday.'

Tio Adolfo nodded approvingly.

An overpowering weariness defeated Jose. It was as if he was falling asleep on his feet. He lay down on the cool wooden floor in the corridor, and placed his hands under his head. He was asleep instantly.

A loud crash ripped him out of it. Another bang and

then another. The back of the house, that's where it came from. No-Name Bird!

A candle burned at the end of the corridor and he could just make out Miguel sitting against the wall, fingers stuck in his ears to cut out the noise. Another crash!

Adolfo's hand was quickly covering his mouth. 'No noise!' he whispered. 'They're shooting from the back.'

'Who?'

'I don't know.'

Pop-pop-pop-pop!

'Lie on the floor and don't move.'

'No-Name Bird!' Jose needed to have the bird with him.

'Shhhhh!' and Adolfo disappeared into the dark. Moments later the bird was in his arms, warm, sweet smelling, No-Name Bird. He gently pecked at Jose's uncovered arm.

Pop-pop-pop. Pale yellow dawn filtered into the house through the cracks in the blinds. Jose was very thirsty but Adolfo allowed him only a few sips from the pannikin.

'What about No-Name Bird?'

'We've trained him well. He does not need water now!'

Pop-pop-pop. On the other side of the house. Men running, shouting. Pop-pop-pop.

Several times Jose heard something whistling through the house. Bullets, he thought. Crockery exploded in the kitchen. Then silence.

'Have they gone?' Jose asked after a while.

'Don't talk!'

No-Name Bird lifted his head, eyes darting about. He sensed something.

Boom-boom-boom. The back door. Someone was trying to break it down. Boom-boom-boom. Wood disintegrating.

Jose pressed No-Name Bird tighter. He felt him protest, trying to wriggle free.

He was afraid now, his tongue flipping in and out of his dry mouth. His heart thumped painfully.

The men were in the corridor, shouting, running from room to room, smashing what little furniture there was.

Someone grabbed Jose by the back of the neck and pulled him up. He was going to cry out but the grip on his neck hurt too much. He felt No-Name Bird fall from his arms. Then he was pushed into the big bedroom where Adolfo and Miguel were standing against the wall, the barrel of a rifle against his uncle's chest.

Jose turned as the hand on his neck let go. The face was so close he felt the man's hot breath. Only it wasn't a man; only a boy, a couple of years older than himself. He vaguely remembered him from school. Like the others, he wasn't dressed in a regular army uniform. Shorts, T-shirts, and sandals were supplemented by Portuguese army caps and ammunition belts; a couple of them wore boots without socks. The boy who had grabbed Jose wore dirty canvas runners, like the tourists wear when they play tennis at the Posada.

One of the older men shoved his rifle into Miguel's throat. Jose saw his stepfather choke. 'Fretilin, Fretilin!' the man shouted, his enraged face touching Miguel's. 'Fretilin soldier, you've been shooting at us!' the man said in Tetum. 'I'm going to cut off your head!'

Miguel had his hands flat against the wall. His face was white and distorted with fear. He whimpered softly.

'He's not Fretilin,' Adolfo said calmly. 'Never Fretilin. Look at him? That's Miguel who drives the truck for Old Wong. People know him in Manututo, in Dili and in Bobonaro.'

'Fretilin, Fretilin!' the man shouted. He wasn't going to lose out.

'Don't hurt him!' Jose suddenly found himself shouting. No-Name Bird too squawked in the corner. 'He's my step-father. You can't hurt him!' His fist struck at the man.

'A fighter, eh?' the older one said, who had a pistol strapped to his belt. He seemed to be in charge. He grabbed Jose by the shoulder and shoved him away. 'It's true,' he said. 'Leave him alone. I know him from Maliana. He drives the truck. He's not Fretilin.' He shifted his rifle. 'Let him go!' Then his face broke into a grin. 'Perhaps we need him to drive the truck to cart away the Fretilin dead.' Everyone laughed, except the man in front of Miguel. His eyes moved from his leader back to Miguel.

A shout outside.

'Let's go!' the older man said.

The man in front of Miguel looked about, unsure of his next move. The others were already running along the corridor towards the back.

With a quick twist of his wrist, the rifle turned sideways and the butt connected with Miguel's ample belly. Jose heard the thud clearly. Like punching into a pillow. Miguel's breath exploded from his body and he crumpled to the floor.

The soldiers were gone. The house was silent except for Miguel's moans.

Adolfo tipped his head and fixed Jose with a stare. 'You were very brave, Jose, very brave.'

Jose realised then that No-Name Bird had somehow managed to move back into the safety of his embrace. He bent his neck and brushed the red comb with his lips.

22

The Flag

Adolfo still kept the blinds over the windows down and the house was very hot in the afternoon. Jose wore only his shorts. Even so, his whole body was wet with perspiration. No-Name Bird too felt the heat, his tiny beak open and gasping in the thick air. Miguel lay on the torn mattress, in the main bedroom besides the broken bed, with a pillow under his head. He had stopped moaning but when Jose brought him water in a cup, he sat up and as he drank he winced in pain.

By the late afternoon the shooting had almost stopped. There was only an occasional pop-pop-pop, but the sounds were a long way off.

'Mamma! Is she safe, Tio? When will she come home?'

'She's safer at the hospital than here. It's better that she remains where she is. There is no safety here.'

Later, Jose lit a candle, for the electricity had gone. He opened some cans of food, serving the cold meat, corn and mixed vegetables in a bowl. He ate with a spoon and drank a little of the water from the pannikin, but he wasn't really hungry. His mother's warm arm around him, that's what he wanted; he wanted things to be normal. Curled up with No-Name Bird beside him, Jose spent an uncomfortable night on the floor of the bedroom between his stepfather and uncle.

He slept in short spells. Once or twice there was some shooting but that too stopped. Some time during the night Jose heard Miguel and Adolfo turn on the Bahasa Indonesian broadcast over Radio Australia, but though it mentioned the fighting between rival political parties, the news was not specific. 'They know little more than we do,' Tio Adolfo had said. Miguel was all for going out to see what was happening, but Adolfo warned against it. 'No one knows who's who in the night. It's better to wait for morning.'

When the sun was up, Adolfo and Miguel pulled the wardrobe away from the front door, and as Jose followed them outside, his eyes ached in the bright light. And he was shocked.

A house further up the road was smouldering, black acrid smoke billowing from the windows and doors. People were standing about, not doing anything – just watching in silence.

And Jose saw the body of a man on the other side of the road, dressed only in black shorts. There was a large red hole in his chest. Adolfo saw Jose watching and put his arm around him. The man's body, especially his legs, were twisted curiously under him, Jose thought, just like those of Angelo de Silva. He wondered if all dead bodies looked the same.

'Don't look, Jose. Death is not for young eyes.'

Miguel started to move along the veranda, but Adolfo held him back. 'What are you doing?'

'We've got to get out.'

'Where to?'

'To the church!'

Adolfo shook his head. 'Better stay here. They won't bother us again.'

Jose heard a noise further up the road. There was a blur of colour, one, two, three, four people coming towards them. Then he recognised Rikki, walking in front, a flag draped over his shoulders. He had it bunched around his body but it was large and the corners trailed on the gravelled road. He had on his pig-skin gloves.

'Adolfo? Adolfo? Heee-ih!' he shouted as he came closer. 'Come with us to the Posada. There are many people there. The soldiers will not harm us. Come with us.'

'The flag, Tio . . .!' Jose began.

'Indonesian!' Adolfo whispered back.

'Apodeti is safety. Come with us, Adolfo, you too Miguel and Jose. Come, come!'

'Is Rikki Apodeti?' Jose asked, incredulous.

'Rikki is not anything. He just hates the Portuguese!'

Rikki paused at the foot of the veranda and looked up at them. His face was covered with fine dust; his black hair was streaked with grey. The others, two Chinese men and Mateo, continued walking in the direction of the Posada.

Jose felt Adolfo move beside him. Then Adolfo shouted: 'We'll come with you, Rikki. We'll come! Wait!' He turned and pushed Jose towards the open doorway. 'Quickly, get your rucksack.'

Jose ran back into the house. No-Name Bird was standing in a corner just inside the doorway, agitated, shifting his weight from one foot to the other. Jose moved past him to his room at the end of the corridor. The cot had been smashed into pieces, also the low chest of drawers. As Jose pulled at the wood it came away in his hand in large splinters. He gasped! Right at the back of the last drawer, he pulled at the rucksack still stuffed with the clothes his mother had packed, also the documents and under the folder, his father's photograph. He picked up the frame. The glass had a few cracks in it. He gently tapped it against the broken bed-head, but not carefully enough for a line of blood appeared on his finger. He sucked at it. Then, with the finger still wet, he took the black-and-white photograph from the frame, rolled it up, and stuffed it into the rucksack's side pocket. One more task! The pack of escudo notes; he squeezed it into the folds of his clothes. Then he rushed back down the corridor, scooping up No-Name Bird, and ran out into the bright light of day.

Rikki and Miguel were already some distance up the road. Adolfo turned and shouted, 'Hurry!' and waved his arm.

With the rucksack bouncing on his back, the bird cumbersome in his arms, Jose raced after them.

23

Marconi

Jose was amazed at the number of people crowded into the Posada. A long corridor, dark corners, and a slightly chilled air which was perfumed with sandalwood – that's what he remembered about the inn from the time when he and Tio Adolfo had gone to give Senhor Jack his money. Now there were men, women and children, many, many of them. Anxious faces peering from crowded rooms, eyes showing hurt, confusion, fear. Children were crying; it was very noisy.

'You can't bring the bird in here!' the man said at the doorway. Jose looked up. It was Old Wong's grandson, Paolo Wei, who now managed the Posada but didn't have the money to keep the pool open or pay Adolfo.

'It's the boy's bird. It must remain!' Adolfo said sternly.

'But not here, Adolfo. There are too many people. If you and your family want to stay, the bird must be kept outside.'

'Come,' Tio Adolfo said to Jose, and pulled him along the corridor. 'We'll find a place for it.'

Out on the wide veranda, Adolfo tied No-Name Bird to one of the posts. 'It'll be safe here,' he assured him.

But Jose wasn't sure. There were a lot of soldiers on the gravelled road and more people were coming towards the Posada, carrying blankets and food. Someone could steal him! 'Don't worry,' Adolfo said and placed a hand on his shoulder.

Inside the Posada, Miguel had organised some blankets for them and they made beds from a couple of old spare cotton cots in the now empty storeroom to one side of the inn's vast kitchen.

As Jose wandered about the corridors, marvelling at just how big the whole place was, he recognised many of the people who had come for the safety the inn offered. Old Wong was there with his many sons and daughters, his grandchildren and great-grandchildren; Jose also saw neighbours, boys from school. And in an open doorway stood Carmillo.

'You've lost the bird!' he said without preliminaries. 'Did they kill it?'

'No, he's outside, tied up.'

'Ah!' Carmillo seemed to brighten up. 'Can we go and have a look?'

'Of course.'

They pushed through the throng of people in the corridor until they stood before the bird on the veranda. He twisted his head to one side and he fixed his bright pebble eyes on Jose, then on Carmillo.

'Its wounds have healed,' Carmillo said.

'Yes!'

Carmillo bent down beside him and stroked the feathers. 'My father said it is very courageous and strong. It will win Adolfo many fights and make a lot of money.'

'He is my bird now!'

'*Your* bird?'

'Yes.'

'You can't fight the bird yourself.'

'The bird doesn't fight! Not any more.'

Carmillo considered this seriously, the skin between his eyes folding into a bulge. 'But the money . . .'

'He is my bird.'

'Will you take it to Portugal with you?'

'Of course,' Jose said without hesitation though he knew it was a lie.

'Has it a name? What do you call it?'

'No-Name Bird.'

Carmillo scratched at his bristly hair. 'No-Name Bird!' He rolled the phrase around his mouth.

Luis and Franco and several of the others from school came onto the veranda to stroke the bird's head. 'Can we walk it around a bit? Just on the veranda?' Carmillo suggested. 'On the string?'

'No, no, no,' Jose shook his head the way Adolfo did: vigorously so that the flesh of his cheeks moved. 'No, he must remain tied to the post. Senhor Wei, the Manager, said so!'

This they understood.

Carmillo tried another way. 'Come with us, Jose?'

'No, no, I must be with Miguel and Adolfo.'

'You don't want to come with us?' Somehow, Carmillo couldn't quite believe it.

Jose felt triumphant. *I've got him*, he thought. 'No, I don't want to come! Not with you, Carmillo!'

Carmillo looked around the circle of faces, disappointed, confused at Jose's refusal. His head dropped and he examined his bare feet. Jose thought: he seemed hurt. One of the others moved away, then another, then the third. Finally, Carmillo got up and made for the front door. He turned. 'We'll be at the back where they used to keep the pigs.'

Jose nodded, then moved his head away to concentrate on the bird. A smile played on his lips. No-Name Bird's eyes glistened. Jose scratched at his throat just under the feathered collar and the bird pressed gently against his fingers.

When he raised his head, Carmillo had disappeared.

Jose straightened up. Fat-head, slob, idiot!

A group of men were talking in the corridor, and as Jose passed he heard them mention Radio Australia. It seemed that everyone was always listening to the broadcasts in Bahasa Indonesian, or in English, Cantonese and Mandarin, and the content was cause for much discussion. 'It's our only source of news,' Adolfo explained. 'You can't really believe what the soldiers tell you.'

The women and children had settled for the night and when Jose entered the storeroom, he found Miguel asleep in the corner, flat on his back, his big belly rising and falling as he snored. There were a few empty bottles of beer beside him. Adolfo was out in the corridor, talking to the men. The floor of the storeroom was polished timber, but by folding the blanket three times, and using the rucksack as a pillow, the makeshift bed did give a measure of comfort.

As he was trying to fall asleep, Jose reached into the side pocket of the rucksack, just under his head, and took out the photo of his father. He didn't want Miguel to see him looking at it so he twisted his body to the side and several times turned furtively, but his stepfather was breathing heavily.

The light was too weak. All Jose saw on the photograph was a vague outline of a head and shoulders, but just holding the print in his hand was comfort enough.

Suddenly there was a commotion out in the corridor. Someone was banging on the front door. People shouting. A woman's voice. Mamma.

Dressed in her nursing uniform, her body was framed in the doorway. With the light behind her, she seemed enormous, formidable. 'Jose? Jose?' she whispered into the room. 'Are you there, my Jose?'

He was up, leaping over Miguel's body, hugging hers, his arms tightly wrapped around her, his head pressing into the soft warmth. Mamma! Mamma!

'You're such a brave young man, just like your father,' she said, holding him now at arm's length. 'Adolfo told me how brave you were when the soldiers came to the house. You didn't cry or were afraid. Oh Jose, I'm so proud of you!'

'Theresa?' Miguel was awake.

Later, after she had eaten rice and canned meat, she sat

between Miguel and Adolfo, her arm still around Jose's shoulders. 'Senhor Jack radioed from the Marconi Centre in Dili today!' She bent down and kissed Jose on the head. 'Fretilin are strong now. It will soon be over.'

'What's Marconi?' Jose asked in a hushed voice.

'That's from where they send radio messages. Fretilin recaptured it yesterday.'

'Fretilin? But what about the soldiers outside. Adolfo said they were Apodeti. They were going to kill Miguel.'

'Hush now. Senhor Jack said the oil plane is ready to come into Baucau. No one knows what's going to happen. Everyone is waiting! Senhor Jack has already picked up the oil people from the south . . .'

Jose's mouth was dry. His stomach felt as though some one had punched him.

'. . . they will radio just before the plane leaves. There is a place for you, Jose . . .'

Jose didn't hear the rest.

Pop-pop-pop-pop. Shooting started again outside.

24

Fretilin

In the afternoon, UDT soldiers dressed in their scruffy, makeshift uniforms came through the front and back doors of the Posada. 'They don't want people to escape,' Adolfo said contemptuously. Miguel hid in the toilets, which had now overflown with use by so many people, and there was no one to clean them.

'Why does Miguel hide in that smelly place, Tio? He's not Fretilin!'

'No, he's just afraid.'

Jose watched as the soldiers rushed from room to room with rags over their faces to protect them from the smell, but they didn't go into the toilets. They took away two men Jose had never seen around Baucau.

While the soldiers were moving about the Posada, Rikki walked around with the flag draped over his shoulders. As the Indonesians were expected by many, it was thought the flag offered some protection.

Jose was surprised when Rikki yelled at the soldiers that there were no Fretilin at the Posada. One of the soldiers pushed him back against the wall with the butt of his rifle. Jose thought he would hit him, but the man shouted, 'It's not your business!' They waved their guns and left. No other people were taken from the Posada.

There was no more shooting that day. Gradually people began to open doors and windows, for the stink made people sneeze and cough. Jose went out onto the veranda to check on No-Name Bird and the first breath of clean air made him retch. No-Name Bird was agitated when he saw him but settled quickly as Jose placed before him a bowl of water and a tiny heap of boiled rice. Then he untied him, but with the string still around his neck he walked him up and down the veranda, the bird exactly one step behind. Several of the men sitting on the Posada steps noticed it and pointed.

'Jose and his little champion,' one said.

'It's his shadow,' said another.

It was as if the bird was oblivious of anyone and anything around him. His place was simply a step behind Jose's feet.

Theresa did not return to the Posada that or the following night, or the one after that. One of the orderlies from the hospital came down to tell Adolfo and Jose that there were so many wounded to take care of she'd decided to sleep in the dormitory. But she did come on the fourth night, and Jose slept beside her, his arm tight around her middle, his face snug in her warmth as usual. They didn't talk much because he noticed her face was grey with fatigue, but being near her, feeling the warmth radiating from her body, that was enough.

She was gone when he woke.

That morning there was a lot of shouting outside the Posada and as the people moved onto the veranda, Jose saw the line of soldiers come down the gravelled road. Jose noticed a few women with the men, also dressed in uniforms.

'Fretilin,' Adolfo said.

'Will they protect us?' asked Jose.

'They are the strong ones now!'

The men and women were dressed in full Portuguese army uniforms and they didn't seem as angry as the UDT soldiers had been. They shouted that all the UDT and Apodeti soldiers had gone. Someone said that Timor had declared its independence in Dili, that there had been a ceremony, with many important people.

Timor was now free.

The Fretilin soldiers were very happy, and laughed and joked with the people at the Posada. The women made coffee and the strong aroma of rabusta mingled with the sharp perfume of clove-flavoured cigarettes. The soldiers mood, however, turned ugly when Rikki appeared with the Indonesian flag still draped around his shoulders. They grabbed him, and one of the soldiers ripped the flag from his body and threw it down on the floor, spitting and stamping on it. Then he slapped Rikki a couple of times around the face. Other soldiers grabbed him and tied his hands behind his back. He was led away. Some of the women and children cried. And Carmillo huddled in a corner, his hands before his eyes, his body shaking.

Tio Adolfo stood with Jose and watched silently. Suddenly Adolfo moved towards the door.

'Open it, open it quickly!' he shouted.

'Why Tio? What are you doing?'

'I must talk to the soldiers. Rikki is clever with his fighting cocks but a *fool* when it comes to politics.'

Then he was gone.

Later, when it was already dark and the people at the Posada were getting ready for the night, there was a loud pounding on the front door. 'It's me, Adolfo,' a voice shouted from outside. 'Let me in!'

One of the men pulled back the bolts, then pushed open the huge wooden panels. People began to emerge from the rooms to see what the noise was all about. Jose was already in the corridor.

Rikki squeezed himself through the front door and behind him was Tio Adolfo, still wearing his hat.

Jose gasped when Rikki's face was illuminated in the poor light of the corridor. His head and shoulders were covered with blood. He didn't have any eyes, only two enormous red and purple bubbles. Jose wondered how he could see at all. His shorts and T-shirt were badly ripped and they looked as if they had been dipped in red paint.

'*Why* did they hurt him?'

'Because he's Apodeti!'

'Is that bad?'

'For Fretilin it is,' Adolfo said and gently pulled at Jose's arm, steering him backwards down the corridor towards the storeroom. Jose suddenly thought of No-Name Bird. He was concerned that all the shouting and noise would have disturbed and frightened him. 'I'll go and see if the bird is all right.'

'It's late, Jose.'

He moved towards the door but Adolfo's hand restrained him.

'They'll have to open the door again. Wait until morning. I'm sure the bird is fine!'

Jose silently mouthed a prayer as he lay on his blanket. He also prayed for his mother and that the soldiers wouldn't take Miguel away and beat him like they had Rikki. The final prayer, just as he slipped into sleep, was for No-Name Bird.

There was no more shooting over the next few days and the Radio Australia broadcasts said that Fretilin had declared independence in Dili, confirming what people already knew.

'Where are the Portuguese people, Tio?'

'They have gone.'

'Does that mean I don't have to go to Portugal now?'

Tio Adolfo looked away. 'There is no future for Timor. You must go to Uncle Carlo in Lisboa.'

'But *why*, Tio?'

'It is best. The Indonesians will come soon. They say Timor belongs to them and they will take it!' Adolfo said angrily.

Many of the people left the Posada to return to their own homes. Adolfo and Miguel had a long talk and when

Mateo left to take one of the sick children up to the hospital, Adolfo told him to tell Theresa that they were going back to the house.

Clutching No-Name Bird and his rucksack, Jose walked behind his uncle and stepfather once more along the gravelled road. A few of the buildings along the way had been burnt and damaged by the fighting, but Jose was still shocked when he moved up onto the veranda of their house and saw what had been done.

The front door had been torn away and there was no glass in the windows. Inside, the furniture was smashed to pieces and had been used to light fires. Empty food cans lay about. Jose retched when he entered his own room; No-Name Bird's wings flapped frantically as he tried to free himself from Jose's arms. The wood from the bed had been burnt in a corner and there was a pile of excrement behind the door. The room was thick with flies and the stench unbearable.

Jose ran back out into the corridor. No-Name Bird wrenched himself from his arms and ran squawking towards the back. Jose dropped his rucksack and vomited against the wall.

'What they have done to the house doesn't matter,' Adolfo's reassuring hand was again on his shoulder. 'It is important that we are not hurt!'

With the cock tied up in the back, the three of them set about removing the rubbish and cleaning the house. The family next door had moved to join relatives at Laga so Adolfo and Miguel dragged across a table, a few chairs and some bedding. Although there were still a lot of the

Fretilin soldiers about, moving up and down the road in pairs or marching to and from the barracks, life began to return to normal. Theresa still lived at the hospital but she came home every couple of days and brought food, mostly canned, from the large supply she said the Portuguese had left behind. People also began to offer vegetables for sale at the marketplace again.

Each night, Adolfo and Miguel sat at the table and at a particular time that Miguel specified, they listened to the crackling Radio Australia broadcast in English and Bahasa Indonesian. They listened only for a short time because Adolfo said the batteries would run down and there was little chance that they could buy more at Old Wong's store. 'The soldiers took everything,' he said.

Jose was intrigued. How could Radio Australia know what was happening in Timor when Australia was such a long way away? 'There are radio people with the Fretilin soldiers up in the hills,' Adolfo explained.

'Australian people?' Jose wanted to know. 'Like Senhor Jack and the Blonde Lady.'

'Like them.'

One night, just after Theresa had left for the hospital, the broadcast seemed of particular interest to Miguel and Adolfo. Their faces yellow from the glow of the lamp, they leaned as close to the radio as they could so they wouldn't miss anything of what was being said. 'What *is* it, Tio?' Jose wanted to know.

When the broadcast had finished, Adolfo turned off the radio and the two men sat silently, their heads bowed.

'Tio? What is it?' Jose persisted.

Adolfo only shook his head. Miguel laid his brow down on his folded arms.

'*Tio?*'

'There is fighting at Balibo. Batugade has fallen. The Indonesians are coming.'

25

Run for the Airport

Adolfo and Miguel talked long into the night, the lamp in the kitchen the only source of light in the house. With the door open, Jose lay on a blanket in the main bedroom, No-Name Bird nestling at his feet. Jose sensed that what Adolfo and Miguel were talking about was of great importance and though he tried to understand the details of what was being said, the men's voices finally made him drowsy and he was soon asleep.

Loud knocking eventually pushed him out of his sleep. It was daylight, and No-Name Bird was pecking at the folds of the blanket looking for food. Someone was banging on the front door and shouting. *The Indonesians are here!* Jose thought.

He grabbed No-Name Bird and peered out of the room. Adolfo was trying to move the door, which still hadn't been fixed properly. It slowly creaked open. Henri da Costa was standing on the veranda. The light hurt Jose's eyes but he could see da Costa waving his arms. He was very excited and kept pointing at the sky. 'They're coming, they're coming!'

The Indonesians, the Indonesians, was all Jose could think of.

Adolfo was beside da Costa. 'Who's coming?'

'The oil plane, the oil plane!' Henri da Costa said. 'Senhora Rodrigus said that Jose must be at the airport in two hours. The radio message said that the oil plane is coming from Dili!'

Adolfo was the first to move. 'Quickly, Jose, get your rucksack! And don't forget the documents.'

'Mamma?'

Henri da Costa dropped his head. 'The Senhora said she could not come!'

'*Mamma can't come?*'

'There are many wounded at the hospital.'

Adolfo pushed him back into the house. 'You must hurry!'

As if enfolded by thick mist, Jose groped about in the mess in the front room until he found his rucksack in the tumble of the blanket. He pulled back the flap over the side pocket. The leather envelope with the documents and his father's photograph were safe. Also the wad of escudo notes.

Miguel was standing on the front veranda, beer bottle in hand. He casually sipped from it with a loud slurp.

'Where's Tio Adolfo?'

'He's gone to the Posada. He will ask Rikki to drive the Land Rover to the airport.'

Jose rushed to the back of the house and untied No-Name Bird. The bird jerked his head about nervously. Jose's stepfather was still standing on the veranda, peering up the gravelled road towards the Posada. Holding the bird firmly in his arms, Jose stood beside Miguel, shifting his weight from one foot to the other. He felt sad and lonely and wished Tio Adolfo would come soon. The man beside him was almost a stranger.

Jose heard the Land Rover before he saw it, the noise of the engine high pitched and occasionally coughing. When it finally came around the bend, a dense cloud of dust followed. Miguel turned and looked down at Jose. 'Goodbye, Jose,' he said in a voice Jose had never heard him use. Still clutching the bottle of beer, he clumsily embraced his stepson. No-Name Bird kicked about. Jose smelled sweat and beer.

Rikki had his head out the window of the vehicle. 'Hurry, Hurry!' he shouted. Jose saw he had the flag around his shoulders again, and on his hands, clutching the wheel, the pig-skin gloves. The door flew open and Adolfo pulled him in with such force that Jose smashed against the back of the seat. As the vehicle lurched forward, No-Name Bird let out a squawk.

Jose was vaguely conscious of the row of houses as they roared up the gravelled road, past the marketplace and the cockpit. A few curious faces flashed past in doorways. As they veered into the road that led to the airport, the Land Rover began to cough and buck. The engine ran smoothly for a short distance, then began again to gasp and wheeze as if it couldn't get enough air.

Rikki kept tapping the instrument panel with his gloved knuckles. 'Petrol, petrol!' he yelled over the din of the engine.

Finally the vehicle lurched forward in one powerful surge, the engine ticking smoothly. Jose saw Rikki slump back, visibly relieved. He turned his head. Jose noticed how swollen his face was, almost distorted out of shape, with dark purple rings under the half-shut eyes.

The airport was in the distance, and there to one side of a small building stood the aircraft, the propellers whirling. Adolfo jabbed his finger at the windscreen. 'Heiiih!' he hissed. There were soldiers all around the plane.

The Land Rover burped and gave one long, drawn-out sigh. The engine died, and slowly the vehicle rolled to a stop.

Silence.

Then Jose became aware of the soft whine of the aircraft's engines in the distance, like the sound the saw made at the back of Old Wong's store when they were cutting wood. Some of the soldiers were waving their arms.

Jose peered at the aircraft through the windscreen. It seemed so far away.

Tio Adolfo reached across Jose and No-Name Bird and pushed open the door. 'Quick, we must go!' Then they were running across the field towards the aircraft, side by side. Adolfo turned his head. Jose had difficulty with the rucksack on his back and the bird in his arms.

'Here, give me the bird!' Adolfo held out his arms.

'No, I'll carry him!'

'Jose, it'll make it easier.'

'No!' He wasn't going to let No-Name Bird go now. He wriggled about, stressed, kicking his feet, claws out. Jose had trouble holding him.

'Run, Jose, run, run, run!'

With Jose still carrying the bird, they raced breathlessly towards the aircraft. The rucksack bounced on Jose's back, then slipped over his shoulder. *I'm going to lose it!* thought Jose in panic, so he twisted his body and pulled it to one side. Holding it hard against his hip so that it would not bounce, he caught up to Adolfo.

Up ahead, the soldiers had taken their rifles from their shoulders and were shouting.

Jose's chest was on fire, excruciating pain in his throat. He wanted to yell to Adolfo that he couldn't run any more, that he had to stop, but Tio Adolfo continued his headlong charge towards the aircraft. Jose was aware of the dust around them as the propeller whirled. The noise of the engines was deafening.

'Tio, Tio . . .!'

'Run, run . . .!' was all Jose heard.

The aircraft was only a little distance away and Jose saw the markings on its side. He recognised the English word 'Oil'.

A big figure appeared from the shadow of the plane at the top of the wooden steps. A big man, with thick arms and a large belly. Jose saw him peer down and grin. He shouted something to the soldiers who moved back from the aircraft. 'Come *on*, Jose, come on. Hurry!' he heard Senhor Jack's voice clearly.

A soldier stood at the foot of the wooden ramp, barring

his way. But Adolfo pushed him aside and to Jose's surprise the soldier stepped back. Jose gripped his arms around No-Name Bird but Tio Adolfo shook his head vigorously and the loose flesh flapped about on either side of his cheeks.

'Tio! Tio!' Jose pleaded.

'No, the bird can't go!' Adolfo grabbed No-Name Bird from him.

Tears dimmed Jose's eyes.

'Here!' Tio Adolfo growled. 'This is part of him.' In a flash of his hand, Adolfo plucked one of the tail feathers from the bird and pressed it into Jose's hand. Then he pushed him onto the first wooden step. 'Go, go, Jose, go, go . . .!' And another whack on his back shoved him upwards. 'Go, go, go . . .!' he heard behind him as he stumbled up the steps, the feather clutched in his wet fist, his other hand tight on the rucksack. There was a thin haze before his eyes, all around him, and he couldn't see properly. As he reached the top, the giant bulk of Senhor Jack loomed before him. An arm reached out and grabbed him by the shirt and pulled him into the dark of the aircraft.

'That's it, let's go!' someone yelled in Portuguese.

Jose blinked about, trying to adjust his eyes. There were people in the plane but he could only make out vague shapes.

'Jose, Jose . . .' a familiar voice. The Blonde Lady. Arms around him, the heavy smell of perfume, soft lips touching his cheeks.

Mamma! Mamma! A voice inside him.

'Tio . . . Adolfo . . . No-Name Bird . . .' he stuttered in Tetum. He wanted to say things but couldn't.

'Don't try to talk,' the Blonde Lady said.

'Tio Adolfo . . .'

The engines of the aircraft erupted and drowned all words. Senhor Jack and another man pulled the door of the aircraft shut. Darkness, only the portholes allowed shafts of light through.

The Blonde Lady helped him pull off the rucksack, then gently pushed him towards a porthole. She was saying something but Jose didn't hear. He peered out. The wooden gangway had been pulled well back and two soldiers stood on either side of it, Tio Adolfo between them, No-Name Bird in his arms.

'Tio? Tio Adolfo!' Jose mouthed and a gut-wrenching sigh shook his body. No-Name Bird, No-Name Bird.

The plane began to move slowly forward. Then it turned and Jose saw a cloud of dust hit Adolfo and the soldiers. The soldiers turned their heads away, but Adolfo stood straight and still, his eyes fixed on the aircraft. A moment later he was gone. Jose saw only the Land Rover with Rikki standing beside it, his gloved hand raised.

The aircraft, with its engines screaming, gained more and more speed. There was a slight lurch and a sensation as if the floor under Jose's feet had dropped. The grey-yellow of the airfield fell away and to one side Jose saw the distant outline of the Mata Bien hills until they too became smaller and smaller. He tried to push his face right up against the window but it was useless. All he could see was blue sky.

Jose turned and looked about. It was like a room crowded with people. Men, women and a few children.

Somewhere at the back a baby was crying. He stood up, holding on to the seat in front. The aircraft was trembling and he had difficulty keeping his balance. A hand pushed him back into his seat. The Chinese man on the other side of the aisle seemed familiar. The man was smiling at him. Chang! He suddenly remembered. The man on the motorbike at Batugade.

'Chang?' he asked softly.

As if he heard him, the man turned his head again and smiled.

The Blonde Lady pointed at something. 'Look! Look!'

Jose leaned forward and squinted through the glass. All he could see was the brilliant blue of the sea below and up over his head the sun dazzled in an explosion of sparks. Then the aircraft dipped its wing to the side and he had a clear view of a long tongue of land, and the sight of it choked his throat.

For an instant he saw his mother's sad, tired face, eyes round with worry and fatigue; the grinning face of Tio Adolfo, his floppy hat pulled to one side, and No-Name Bird with his blood-red comb swaying as he pecked at his fingers through the wire mesh of the crate. Then, outside, a dense cloud of white suddenly enveloped the plane and the images were gone.

Jose turned his head and blinked into the half-light of the aircraft's interior.

The Letter from Timor

Quickly, Doctor Rodrigus read over the large, carefully constructed words. His mother's handwriting was becoming larger and larger to the point where a line held only a few words. Her eyesight was failing. It was good that she had her sister Amelia to look after her.

But when he read the sentence which began, '. . . we've heard from the International Red Cross again and they have confirmed that Tio Adolfo was killed in the fighting at Bobonaro . . .' his heartbeat thumped heavily. Tio Adolfo. Tio. You have gone back to your Tree of Life, he thought. With all the fighting in Timor, clans warring against clans, village against village, neighbours taking guns to each other all for the sake of political expediency, it is fitting that you my uncle should end your life where it had all begun.

He got up from the chair and with the letter in one hand, the paperweight in the other, he moved to the window. He thought of his uncle, of his No-Name Bird, of his Mamma.

The rest of the letter was filled with his mother's usual plea to return to Timor. 'I'm getting older, Jose mio, and God will not be kind to me too much longer.' But even though conditions in Timor were changing rapidly, Jose's work with Amnesty International, his work in seeking an independent Timor, would make such a visit impossible.

Mamma. It was something they both understood. And he looked once again at the paperweight, with its beautiful irridescent cock's feather, and thought of home.

About the author

Josef Vondra was born in Vienna, Austria, and came to Australia when he was ten years old. He spent fourteen months at a migrant camp in New South Wales where he learnt his first words of English. On moving to Melbourne, he had his first short story published at the age of fifteen.

Jo has worked variously in journalism, including a cadetship with the *Sun News Pictorial*, as a sub-editor with Radio Australia, a columnist with the *Age* and as a contributor to various newspapers and magazines, including *Reader's Digest*. With fellow Radio Australia journalist, Graeme Turpie, Jo was the first newsman to be allowed full travelling rights within Portuguese Timor.

No-Name Bird began as a newspaper feature story, and draws heavily on Jo's own experience in Timor. Jo has also written a number of travel books, including *Timor Journey*, published in 1967. His first novel, *Paul Zwilling*, was published in 1974, and he was awarded a Senior Writer's Fellowship through the Australia Council the following year.

Jo now lives in Lorne, on Victoria's Great Ocean Road. He has a daughter Ally, and runs his own magazine publishing business.